MW00736960

ISSUE FIVE
WINTER 2010

Minnetonka Review is proud to be environmentally conscious. This issue is printed on Finch Casa Opaque 30% post-consumer recycled fiber, which is chlorine free and produced in a factory that utilized 66% renewable fuels. Finch is certified by the Sustainable Forest Initiative and has a partnership with The Nature Conservancy.

Minnetonka Review is an independent journal published twice annually on Lake Minnetonka, one of the largest lakes in Minnesota. The lake was first discovered by two children paddling up Minnehaha Creek from Fort Snelling. In 1852, Minnesota's territorial governor, Alexander Ramsey, named the lake after hearing the native Dakota people refer to it as minn-ni-tanka, which means "Great Waters." Soon thereafter, the first hotel was built on its shores and in 1855, Henry Wadsworth Longfellow made the area famous with his epic poem, "The Song of Hiawatha." Minnehaha, the heroine of his poem, was named after the creek that flows from Lake Minnetonka to become a tributary of the Mississippi. Minnehaha is the word for waterfall, or "laughing waters."

Minnetonka Review accepts unsolicited manuscripts from Oct. 15th to May 15th. Send up to 6,000 words of prose or 8 poems to: *Minnetonka Review*, P.O. Box 386, Spring Park, MN 55384, or save the paper and postage and submit through our online submission manager. We are not responsible for lost manuscripts. For the latest guidelines, visit: www.minnetonkareview.com.

Cover Art: Keith Demanche
Typset and Interior Design: Troy Ehlers

Photograph of Mark Spitzer and alligator gar copyright Eric Tumminia.

The photographs in "The Twin Cities a Century Ago" are public domain, photographers unknown. The newsclippings and ads therein were published in the *St. Paul Daily Globe* and acquired from the Library of Congress, who in turn acquired them from the Minnesota Historical Society. Thanks to Bob Hurner for access to his collection.

Minnetonka Review

Editor in Chief
Troy Ehlers

Art Director
Keith Demanche

Poetry Editor
Jamie Ellis

Non-Fiction Editor
M. Stephen Anderson

Fiction Editor
Troy Ehlers

Advisory Editors
Tim Salyers
JoAnn F. Cox
Rachel Ackland
Alexis Bergman

ISSUE FIVE
WINTER 2010

FICTION

NONFICTION

POETRY

EDITOR'S PRIZE AWARDS

The Minnetonka Review

Editor's Prize

For Prose

Stephen Graf

"Hadamard's Billiards"

Brandon Krieg

"Prodigal"
"Squaw Fish"
&
"Inversion among the fish counters at Bonneville dam"

For Poetry

The Editor's Prize generally recognizes writers who've not published a major book by awarding $150 to one prose and one poetry author from each issue.

Foreword

Sometimes a writer has a page sitting in front of him—a *blank* page—and he struggles to come up with the words to fill it. Even worse, maybe he's an editor with a foreword to write, a space he needs to fill not because he feels artistically inclined, but because he's obligated. Obligated to meet a deadline, no less. Maybe the battle has been escalating for quite some time, from an innocuous item on a to-do list to a lingering dread, and climaxing in the frenzied final moments before the issue goes to print.

He tells himself there's nothing to it. He's a writer, dammit! This is his job. He lives for filling the page with ink, for turning a crafty phrase; conjuring an image; conveying thought through words. So what's his problem? There are excuses, sure... His craft is writing *fiction*, not forewords! He doesn't even *believe* in forewords, never reads them in other journals. Maybe that's it, he tells himself: he just hasn't read enough to know what to put in them... So he grabs some journals from the shelf and—*wait a minute*—most of them don't even *have* editor's notes! Why is he even bothering then? Who was it that told him he needed to do this? Nobody reads forewards. He could just skip it... But *no!* There's already a blank page waiting in the layout!

It's not as if there aren't things to write about. He could comment on the journal's fine stories and poems. Except he believes they should stand on their own; nothing he could say would improve upon them. From the journal's century-old photos, he could spin off an essay about how times change and yet stay the same. No, that's lame. (Although it *does* seem funny they were selling penis enlargement devices in the 1800s (p. 108)). He could rail on about how not enough people are reading books, or he could give a chest-thumping pep-talk filled with rally cries about how there will *always* be room in the world for great literature. *Semper Libri!*

As a last resort, the editor could just write a whole page about how he needs to fill that page, like how the Kaufman Brothers did with the Nicolas Cage/Meryl Streep film *Adaptation*. But if he was so bold, so desperate, so time-pinched, to resort to such trickery, he would be feeling insecure by the last lines—wondering how hokey this will seem; will it look like he's full of himself? That he thinks he's funny? How dare he waste everybody's time with such vacuous writing?

I have no idea how the writer will solve this dilemma, but I suppose he'll manage somehow. Writers can be very resourceful.

—Troy Ehlers, *Editor in Chief*

Stephen Graf

Hadamard's Billiards

*Jacques Hadamard is considered by many to be the first dis-
coverer of chaos. In 1898, Hadamard published an influential
study entitled "Hadamard's Billiards" in which Hadamard was
able to show that all trajectories are unstable, in that all particle
trajectories diverge exponentially from one another.*

MY EARS WOULDN'T STOP RINGING, that was the first
thing I noticed. As I walked, I could barely control my gait; I'd
lost all sense of balance. It reminded me of the feeling I used to get when
I was a kid and would spin around until it made me so dizzy I had to
drop to the ground. With each new step, I felt I would tumble face-first
into the pavement, into the blackness. But I pressed forward, not under-
standing why, or even where I was going. I just knew I had to get away.

*A meteorologist named Edward Lorenz was the first true ex-
perimenter in chaos theory. In 1960, he was working on the
problem of weather prediction. Lorenz had a computer set up
with a set of twelve equations to model the weather. The predic-
tions could not be 100% accurate, but the program was able to
theoretically predict what future weather might be.*

Maria had told me before we vacationed there the first time that San
Sebastian was the most beautiful city in the world. Her parents had taken
her there as a kid when Franco was still in power and used to spend his
summers there. There was something magical about it, she insisted, and

upon seeing it I had to agree. Nestled between a set of green mountains and the Bay of Biscay in the Basque region of northern Spain, when the sun shines there, which is usually, one can't help thinking that if there was a god, *this* was what he was thinking when he created the earth. The rest of the planet was just practice. The town itself was a cross between a quaint nineteenth century fishing village, and a more modern resort town. Maria and I had come here for our first official holiday as a couple, a few months after we'd started dating, so it held a special place in both of our hearts. When I decided to ask her to marry me, I knew it had to be here.

Like other small towns in Spain, the townspeople still turned out and promenaded the plazas every Saturday night. So as I staggered wildly down the sidewalk, couples in their finest clothes had to step aside to give me room. They stared at me as they did so, and some of them spoke to me, but I couldn't hear them because of the ringing in my ears. I felt like I was enclosed in one of those plastic bubbles, where nothing could touch me, and I could touch nothing. This feeling was put to the test by a stout woman with iron-gray hair and a brown shawl who refused to yield to some drunken foreigner weaving his way down the street. I thought I was going to ram her for sure, causing my bubble to burst and leaving the two of us sprawled on the dirty, cobblestone street. But at the last second, through a supreme effort, I was able to veer to the right, barely eluding her.

> *One day in 1961, Lorenz wanted to see a particular weather sequence again. In order to save time, he started the program in the middle of a sequence instead of at the very beginning. When he returned an hour later, the pattern had evolved differently, diverging from the earlier result, ending with a wildly different configuration from the original.*

Maria always said we were blessed, and I never argued with her. But I had my misgivings. When those bombs went off in the Madrid Metro a couple years back, I was supposed to be there. What I mean is the one bomb went off at my stop at the time when I normally would have been there. I'd been at the Atocha station at exactly seven-thirty every week-day morning since I'd started work at a public relations firm in Madrid a year earlier. But that morning, I'd forgotten an important document I'd taken home to work on the previous night. Cursing my absentmindedness, I rushed back to my flat to get it. By the time I returned to the vicinity of the station, the three bombs had already detonated, leaving the surrounding area shrouded in smoke—blanketed in thick layers of dust, grief and turmoil. When I saw Maria that evening, she threw herself on me and wouldn't let go, as though she was trying to make sure I wasn't some sort of apparition that would evanesce the moment she released me. She kept saying it was a miracle. I preferred to think it was luck, because there was no miracle for those 191 people that did show up at their stops on time that day. It's difficult to accept that the only difference between a miracle and tragedy might be a little timing.

After that, Maria said we had to live each day like it might be our last. She always had anyway; she was so impulsive and full of life. And I tried to be like that, too. For a few weeks I tried, walking around filled with excitement and wonder, the way I had when I first moved to Madrid from the States. But it's hard to live that intensely for one month, let alone an entire lifetime. So gradually, as the city around me began to heal and fall into its old, regular patterns, I did the same. People have short memories. They have to. Otherwise, how could anyone ever get out of bed in the morning, knowing that everything around us is uncertain? Its existence in a constant state of flux, the entire human race is menaced with the possibility of sudden and unalterable change at every moment of every day; continually oppressed by the grim specters of pain and death. We are surrounded by chaos, so we make sense of it as best we can.

> *The phenomenon Lorenz discovered—one of two main components of what came to be known as chaos theory—was sensitive dependence on initial conditions, although it is more commonly referred to as the "butterfly effect."*

People who live through tragedies like the Madrid bombings, or the 9/11 attacks in New York—even if it is only tangentially like my experience—

become identified as survivors. But when I analyze this kind of categorization, taking it to its ultimate conclusion, then it seems to me it becomes reductive to the point of absurdity. After all, isn't everyone who is living a survivor in some sense? And if everyone is a survivor, then it basically splits human existence into two camps, both of which everyone will occupy eventually—those who survived, and those who didn't. Why, then, this urgency to live life differently?

Nevertheless, for a time we tried. One of the first things we did was to take that first trip together to San Sebastian. The day we arrived we took a tour in a taxi-cab and the driver had pointed out to us a splotch on the side of a cliff where—according to legend—an ETA terrorist had accidentally blown himself up while trying to plant a bomb years earlier. Maria was a pacifist to the point that she wouldn't kill a spider that was terrifying her in our apartment. And she wouldn't let me kill it either. Instead, I had to find a way to scoop it up in a newspaper, and take it outside to set it free. Which I did, with a resounding "splat" as soon as Maria was out of earshot. I remember Maria rhetorically asking the taxi driver why anyone would want to set off a bomb in the most beautiful place on earth. As though the beauty or ugliness of the setting made any difference.

Beauty means nothing to a bomb. A bomb accomplishes its work the same regardless of the aesthetic value of its surroundings. In a sense, a bomb operates much like chaos theory. The results are unpredictable and utterly chaotic, yet there is an underlying order to it. A bomb is utilitarian in nature; its job is simply to explode. The success or failure of the bomb itself is predicated on that and that alone. What causes a bomb to be considered good or bad is the use it is put to, and who is judging it. If it frees a group of trapped coal miners, the bomb is good. If it goes off in a crowded commuter bus, to most people it's bad—except to the terrorists who planted it. So it all depends on perspective.

The butterfly effect dictates that a very minor change in the initial conditions can drastically change the long-term behavior of a system. Therefore, as Lorenz later put it, just one flap of a butterfly's wings in Brazil could result in a tornado in Texas.

When I first started dating Maria, I remember her asking me if I had ever heard of "la teoria de chaos." Because my Spanish still wasn't very good then, and because the way she pronounced the Spanish *chaos* sounded exactly like the English word *cows*, I thought she had asked me if I had ever heard of the *theory of cows*. I burst out laughing, and she couldn't understand why. All I could imagine was a group of cows, standing together in a field out in the country somewhere, lowing contentedly as they chewed their cuds and stared off blankly into space. I don't remember why she'd asked me about that—neither of us were scientists, or even scientifically inclined. All I remembered was the theory of cows. And in a sense, it wasn't a bad theory. Those cows in my mind's eye were contented, even happy in their way, oblivious to the fact that any day might end with them on the floor of a slaughterhouse. It wasn't really a theory, more of an image, but that was all right.

After that conversation, I looked the theory up on the Internet—the theory of chaos, that is, not cows. It seemed like a lot of it had already entered the common lexicon, as eventually happens with scientific discoveries. I read that many scientists believed that twentieth century science would be remembered for only three theories: relativity, quantum mechanics, and chaos. Aspects of chaos surround us: from the flow of blood through blood vessels, to a tree's branches, to the currents of the ocean, to the effects of turbulence. What surprised me was that the type of chaos which chaos theory dealt with was not the madness of the Madrid train bombings, or scenes like what I'd just lived through, but rather an orderly, even predictable kind of chaos.

But maybe the theory of chaos is simply another human construct that we try to lay over life in order to make some sense of it. Where I really think the chaos resides is inside of all of us. We are at all times consumed by contradictions—love, hate, happiness, sorrow, desire, revulsion—and these paradoxes are constantly at war with one another. What results is chaos. Not the orderly, predictable chaos of the chaos theory, but the unmitigated anarchy of the soul. How else can one explain someone setting off a bomb in a hotel in the most beautiful place on earth, randomly killing everything nearby?

The human heart has a chaotic pattern. The time between beats does not remain constant; it depends on how much activity a person is doing, among other things. The heartbeat can speed up under certain conditions. Under other conditions, the heart beats erratically. It has even been called a chaotic heartbeat.

This time it was Maria who'd forgotten something and had to go back, only this time it wasn't lucky. Standing on the wide veranda that ran along the front of the hotel, I watched her as she bounced through the glass doors and made her way across the lobby toward the elevators. Moments later I saw the lobby fill with flames. It was one of those unreal moments, where one sees clearly what is occurring, but one cannot believe it is truly happening, as though it were all part of some terrible dream. But this wasn't a dream. The sound came a split second later; it was a deafening roar that seemed to consume every other sound, like a black hole. This was followed immediately by a concussive blast that blew me from the porch, like a leaf caught in the wind. Landing on the sidewalk on the other side of the street, nearly ten meters from where I'd originally been standing, I was momentarily rendered unconscious.

When I came to, I couldn't hear anything, not a sound. Then the ringing gradually commenced, low at first but louder as it went. Turning to the hotel, I saw flames licking out of the ground floor windows, and dazed and bloody people beginning to stagger out. I watched for Maria, but she didn't come. In a haze, I ran my hands along my arms and legs to feel if there were any bones poking out. I wiped my face to feel for blood, but there was none. I pulled myself to my feet and limped toward the front door.

The analysis of a heartbeat can help medical researchers find ways to put an abnormal heartbeat back into a steady state, instead of uncontrolled chaos. It has been speculated that the human brain might also be organized somehow according to the laws of chaos.

The inside of the hotel was like a scene from Dante's *Inferno*. Acrid, black smoke billowed in the air, making it almost impossible to breathe. Half of the ceiling had collapsed. Broken furniture and bodies were strewn about the lobby floor. Along with the smoke and the dust, the air was filled with the moans and the shrieks of the survivors, which somehow pierced the ringing in my ears. I found Maria, what was left of her, in the back of the lobby near the elevators. She must have been close to the original blast, judging by the state of her. At least she went quickly—probably didn't even have time to realize what was happening. One second she's skipping through the lobby to retrieve her lipstick, and the next she finds herself launched into eternity.

I gathered up her body and carried it out to the street and lay it by a group of the wounded, huddled on the sidewalk in front of the hotel. I would have kissed her face goodbye, but there was nothing left to kiss. The bomb had taken care of that. I straightened up and began to stumble away from the scene. I thought I saw someone call to me, but I couldn't make out what he said, and didn't really care, either. At first I just fled. I had to get away and it didn't matter where. Then I noticed the chaos of my flight had an underlying order. I was heading for the beach at La Concha Bay. It was there I was going to propose to Maria that evening.

> *The chaos theory is paradoxical in nature. Although chaos is often thought to refer to randomness and lack of order, it is more accurate to think of it as an* apparent *randomness that results from complex systems and interactions among systems. Thus, the chaos theory is really about finding the underlying order in apparently random data.*

As I got closer to the beach, my hearing began to gradually return. People dressed in their Sunday's best were rushing past me toward the columns of smoke that were rising from the hotel. I clearly heard the word, "sangre" from one onlooker, and a man with a concerned look on his face asked me in halting English, "Señor, are you okay?" I ignored all of this and kept walking.

Stephen Graf

The way a bomb works is it can't take away your memories of a person, and it can't rob you of your past. But it can wipe out your future in a matter of seconds. And not only your future, the futures of the children you would have had, and their children. The aftermath is exponential, like the butterfly effect—like chaos.

When I got to the bay, the tide was out. The sun was beginning to set and the water was so calm it looked like a deep blue sheet of glass. I could hear the wailing of police and ambulance sirens from the town center. Before me the beach was completely deserted; the commotion caused by the explosion had cleared off the last stragglers. I took a couple dozen wobbly steps onto the beach, and then dropped to my knees in the soft, white sand in front of a small pool of sea water that had been left behind by the receding tide. I wanted to cry or scream or do something to let out this emotion that was bottled up in me, but I couldn't. I was numb.

Digging in my jacket pocket, I produced the box containing Maria's ring. Removing the ring, I let the box drop into the sand in front of me. I tried to hold the ring up so I could look at it in the golden rays of the setting sun. But my hands were shaking so badly it slipped from my grip and dropped into the shallow pool in front of me without a ripple. Glancing down, I was able to make out my reflection on the surface of the pool.

I was covered in blood.

It wasn't mine.

Alexandria Marzano-Lesnevich

Stuck

ELLIE HAD HER FINGER STUCK UP HER NOSE when I met her. She was leaning over the adhesion tester so all I could see was blond hair and a lab coat, but I knew that stance. I'd done it before myself, twisting my finger like a corkscrew to work the glue in higher when a straight sniff didn't cut it anymore. "Careful you don't get stuck that way," I said, and she laughed, and wouldn't you know it, it did stick. Cyanoacrylate-54, a swift kick of a high but a pretty dumb move. Your nostril's lined with soft, delicate hairs and man, those fuckers hurt when you pull them.

Wasn't long after that we started messing around. The factory had been a hospital back in the days of bricks and ether, and had plenty of gloomy little rooms full of abandoned equipment, places no one would find us. I knew them all. I was an old-timer by glue factory standards. I'd started working there in high school, spending my summers testing samples on machines that looked like something Dr. Frankenstein would have used to squirt the elixir of life into his dear old monster, all syringes and metal springs. Six months of college in a pretty little town with a green in the middle, then my mom got sick and I moved back home to take care of her. The factory gave me back my old job, this time with the title of research technician, a fancy name for something a monkey in a lab coat could've done. Four years later I was still there, pushing the same levers and testing the same samples from the scientists, who were still trying and failing to find a knock-off for Post-It notes. It's the Holy Grail of adhesives. Everyone wants to be able to undo what they've just stuck.

Alexandria Marzano-Lesnevich

When Ellie wasn't around I'd hang out in the lab and read. Dickens, Golding, Brontë. The orphan classics, I guess you'd call them. My lab coat had wide, deep pockets that could hide a paperback, and I rigged a pencil to hang off my right cuff with yet another failed Post-It knock-off, one that was too strong for paper—caused substrate failure and the sheet ripped—but if you wanted to hold onto something a little heavier it was perfect. I showed Ellie the pencil trick and she taught me to make bandages out of just about anything: paper, the condoms I carried in my other pocket, once an old rag she'd asked me to tie around her mouth like a gag. If you'd seen us back then you would've thought we'd barely survived an accident, we were taped up better than any crash victim.

It was pretty hard to get fired from a place where half the staff was high, but even by those standards Ellie was pushing it. She started to have a look to her like the fat lip of a dead fish, too glass-eyed to care about the hook. I figured she had to be screwing our supervisor, too, but she didn't volunteer and I didn't ask. It's not like I was a shining star myself. The bills from the funeral were coming in, I was shooting and snorting my paychecks as quick as I got them, and it was starting to look like the only way I'd ever make it back to college was as the old guy in the back of the class, the one who everyone figures is just there to ogle the coeds. Maybe I'd slip a little glue onto their skirts, see some skin that way.

So it wasn't a total surprise when one afternoon, after a particularly satisfying fuck in a supply closet, Ellie said she wanted to come back that night and clear Accounts Receivable out. I pulled a paper clip off her ass where it'd gotten stuck and then kissed the red welt it left behind, feeling the chemical residue burn my lips. She had an ass that should've been cast in copper and made into a monument, something unbreakable and forever.

I'd never seen the factory totally dark before, all the machines silent. Ellie took a key out of her pocket and soon enough I thought we were done, but she slipped her hand down my pants and led me into the lab. One last goodbye go of it, I thought. Ellie had other ideas. She climbed up on the lab desk, the same one we both work over, and started kicking at the window. She still had on the steel-toed boots we're required to wear, the one management lets us pick off a company truck once a year like it matters what style you get when they're all butt-ugly, but even so the glass wouldn't break. Cracks spread like spiderwebs, they etched up the glass until it looked about as strong as my mother had those last months, but still it didn't shatter. "You're never going to bust it, Ellie," I said. I knew. I'd helped paint the safety resin on the window myself. But standing there, watching her throw her small body at the glass, seeing how hard she tried and how hard it stayed, something inside me gave. I picked up the adhesion tester and hurled it at the window and what do you know, that sucker broke clean through.

Eli Langner

The Koi of Nijo

they glide through mossy water
undulating spindles spun of silk
glinting through the murky veil
swirling daubs of spectral glow:
orange, yellow, white and ruby
clustered as their need requires
separate as their dappled marks

Utsuri is calico coral and coal
Ochiba Shigure is fallen leaves
Shiro Bekko, footprints in snow
Kumonryu wears a black jacket
Tancho, a red spot on his head
Aka Matsuba is copper pinecone
Yamabuki Ogon is woven gold

they cannot see their own beauty
only the kaleidoscope of others
and the errant bugs and blossoms
left drifting on the silvery surface;
they can only swim in lazy circles
fins their only means of motion
round and round the castle moat

Bart Galle

Emblem

Two boys outside the bookstore, smoking
on a cold spring day. Their long scarves
swing back and forth as they move their feet
from spot to spot, as if no place will have them.

Their faces are fresh, and they laugh
at things they say and spit occasionally,
watching it with some interest. I can't help
but love them and have the urge

to wish them well in their struggle.
When one of them leans back and yawns,
I can almost picture it tipping into
an existential howl, but instead I am reminded

of my cockatiel, stretching her wings dramatically
when I walk in the door, as if to say to me,
I haven't missed you. I've been sleeping
the whole time you've been gone.

Bart Galle

Your Painting of an Iris, Unfinished

I'd like to say the blossom is there
without the supporting structure;
that, typical of youth,
there was a rush to fulfillment,
followed by a loss of interest.
But no.
The leaves and stems are complete
and carefully rendered
in icy blue-greens
and mottled ochres. A bud
is finished, as is a lesser flower
in the lower right
designed to balance
the full one in the upper left.
That's the one left undone.
The outer petals are finished,
some in a saturated purple,
others in a pale blue wash,
but the heart of it is blank,
just penciled in, a gaping hole
right where our eyes
are forced to go.

Edward H. Fischer

Matterhorn Dreams

(...and where they might take you)

I MET THE TWO GERMANS on the trail north, above Trift. There were only four of us en route to the Mettlehorn. If there were any others I'd have seen them as I was on that goat-path most of the day. I had come for the Matterhorn but by then, on our next to last day in Switzerland, had given it up. The Mettlehorn was for consolation. It isn't much compared to the Matterhorn. Still, getting up there is a feat, its summit more than a vertical mile above the village. I had never been so high except in an airplane, and I had no technical climbing experience, yet had come hoping to try the Matterhorn.

Long before I'd heard it described as "...mostly a walkup." I had no interest in mountaineering then but that tantalizing (and *misleading*) phrase had stuck with me and now, twenty-some years later, I'd begun to think I needed just such an adventure to get me by one of life's long gray periods. I was about to turn fifty. Recently I had switched from a dreary job to an exasperating one. I was doing little that I enjoyed and accomplishing nothing important to me. If I were ever going to try a big mountain it had better be soon and so, in late summer of 1984, my wife Cathy cooperating with the whim, we took a charter flight and trains, by way of Zurich, to Zermatt.

The first day we hiked from Schwarzee to the Hörnli hut, the starting point for the usual and easiest route up the mountain. We talked with an American who'd been to the top that morning. Young and lean, he didn't look especially whipped but was limping, his leg muscles already stiffening. He had attempted the climb four years earlier but had to quit, exhausted when he reached the Solvay Refuge, an emergency shelter located at 13,000 feet. This time he'd trained there for two weeks, hiking or climbing every day. He said the highest sections of the Hörnli ridge were grueling. Near the summit he'd experienced an out-of-body sensation that he blamed on fatigue and altitude. He shook his head, it hadn't been worth it. I was having doubts.

The weather that week was a determining factor, clouds and rain more prevalent than sun. It never rains on the Matterhorn, I was told. It only snows. Until it burns off, the fresh snow makes the climb too strenuous. On two of those rainy days we took the train to Berne for some city life. Finally with only a day left I had to settle for the Mettlehorn.

I spotted the first German on the knoll above Trift. In Zermatt you see lots of tourists, many of them German, costuming as alpinists: middle-aged, stocky, ruddy-faced men and women in heavy boots, knee-high stockings, and drab climbing knickers. Their backpacks are full and some carry ice axes, but you have the feeling the paraphernalia is for show, and that these folks don't stray far from the shops and restaurants. This man—in his early forties, dark hair, lanky build—didn't fit that stereotype, and he seemed to know what he was doing so I asked him if the trek to the Mettlehorn was hard going, as I'd heard. "No... it is an easy tour," he said, speaking precisely, setting his mind to English. We went on together for awhile. He let me know my pace was too quick so I adjusted it to his.

Two others came along: a Swiss who spoke no English sailed past, too fast for either of us; and an older man, another German, closed in on us as we approached a ridge spanning two peaks. I guessed all three had spent the night in the old farmhouse-lodge at Trift, starting out fresh that morning, saving themselves a couple of hours hiking up the steep ravine from Zermatt. According to the first German the peak to our right was our destination. It was closer than I expected. We had to cross a sloping snowfield to reach the col. From there the ridge led to the summit.

I took off my pack to look for gloves. The two Germans started across the snowfield, traversing it with no difficulty. I approached it cautiously, afraid of a sudden ride down-slope. The older German called over to check that I was all right.

When I reached the col I saw the first German near the top. The Swiss was already coming down. The ridge was clear but the summit dome held about an inch of new snow. I climbed carefully, using handholds where I could. As I came near the top the German directed my moves. He seemed glad to see me.

"You have made it," he said. "But I have bad news—it is not the Mettlehorn." He was studying a topographic map, and showed me where we'd gone wrong. We were on the Platthorn; the Mettlehorn was more to the north, higher and steeper than the Platthorn. We could see the trail-line we should have taken. Far below, it crossed another big snowfield, then zigzagged up the southern face of the Mettlehorn. We followed the progress of the other German. He'd taken the correct route but after negotiating two or three switchbacks, was coming back down. "He has no crampons," my companion explained.

In the other direction the massive, tilted hammerhead of the Matterhorn soared over an unbroken platform of clouds, a magnificent sight.

"It's the most spectacular thing I've seen in nature," I told him.

"I would assume so," he replied. Then, as if he had sensed the conde-scension of his remark, he added, "It is also the most spectacular thing I have seen."

I asked him if he'd thought of climbing it. No, it was a techni-cal climb—therefore not for pedestrians like us, was the implication. Considering we hadn't even made it to the Mettlehorn, I had to agree.

I took out a snack, and he withdrew a small notepad and pen, and began to write in tiny meticulous lines. Recording his impressions of the site, I imagined. Truly Germanic. Then he produced a camera and began adjusting it, presumably for a shot of the Matterhorn. I suggested a picture of him with the 'horn in the background. He seemed reluctant to put his camera in the hands of a stranger but I could see he liked the idea. The opportunity to be photographed pricked his vanity. He removed his hat, slicked his hair, and posed on the edge of the rock, crossing his legs and forging a smile.

As the clouds moved up he prepared to leave. Hurriedly I gathered my stuff, not wanting to be left up there with poor visibility. I dogged his steps going down. We saw the other German now coming up the Platthorn, seeking that one peak for his efforts. He and his countryman exchanged phrases across the slope.

At the col I unshouldered my pack again to get a drink, and was stunned to find the upper compartment open and my wallet missing. It didn't contain much money but my driver's license and credit cards were in it, somewhere on top. "You must go back," said the German. This I knew but, weary, I dreaded having to go up there again and having to cross that snowfield late in the day.

The other German was hollering something from above. The first answered, using his hands as a megaphone. I heard the word "fantastic," and supposed they were discussing the view. But it was my wallet. "He has found it," the first German said. "You only have to wait here and he will bring it to you." Delighted, I shook his hand. He said we might meet again in the village but I didn't see him again.

The other German was blond and heavyset, friendlier than the first, more spontaneous, and his English more fluent. As he approached he sang in German, then in English: "I—have—your—mon-ey." As he hand-ed me the wallet I offered him all the cash in it, forty Swiss francs, but he refused, saying he had plenty of money.

We descended to the snowfield and crossed it with ease. I knew the rest of the way would be uneventful, merely a long trudge back down to the alleys of Zermatt.

"There it is. Oh, wow. Wow-wow-wow!"
(Woman overheard on terrace of Zermatt hotel, on first sight of the Matterhorn.)

We ended the vacation in Italy. I reasoned that my affair with the Matterhorn was over too but, back home, the idea of climbing it began to haunt me again. That fall I took a rock climbing lesson, did poorly, but was only momentarily deterred. I spent half a day at the American Alpine Club—located in New York City, at that time—and on a trip to London in May, put in equivalent time at the British Alpine Club library, searching for information about the Hörnli Ridge route and the feasibility of the climb for a beginner. I conferred by phone with John Jenkins who with little experience had scaled the Matterhorn and written about it for the *New York Times*—and with Alphonse Franzen, a 61 year old Swiss guide who reportedly had been up it more than 500 times. I was pretty sure I'd go back. I bought a rope and harness, some carabiners and an ascender, and practiced until I was confident on elementary rock routes. By early summer I had made travel and hotel arrangements and was working out almost every afternoon, alternating days of jogging, rock climbing, and scrambling up and down a 400 foot slope near work.

On July 20 I left for Switzerland, traveling alone this time, although I was joined there by Amerigo ("Mig") Farina, a friend who hiked with me for five days (on one of those training days we went up the Mettlehorn, the summit that had eluded me and the two Germans the year before). I met with Alphonse Franzen, the effusive guide I had phoned from the States. With his beer-barrel physique, fisherman's cap, flashing eyes, and sun-burnt face he had the appearance, as Mig later observed, of a rogue pirate. We discussed the preliminary climbs and workouts I'd have to do—some with him, some on my own—to prepare for the Matterhorn. Much of Franzen's time was taken by a wealthy German woman who climbed all season long and provided him the luxury of helicopter lifts up to the huts and climbing sites. His routine clients had to be worked in around her outings which took many of the finest days.

That first week we climbed the Rifflehorn, a small mountain used for practice and tryouts. After he had belayed me through a few moves at the start he muttered, more to himself than to me, "I will take you on the Matterhorn." Of course I was thrilled to hear that. My modest climbing routines on home crags had paid off.

After I had passed all of his tests on rock, ice, and at altitude I had to wait for an opening in his schedule and suitable weather. It was a tense period because my vacation was melting away quickly. I didn't like thinking this but he kept reminding me, I still might not get my chance. I spent part of a brilliant afternoon up behind the Hörnli Hut, watching climbers come off the mountain. A path across a snowfield leads to the headwall where the actual ascent begins. Here, in a recess in the wall, sits a life-size Madonna, paid for by the German lady, Alphonse told me. Coming past the statue, having made the top, the climbers looked flushed, bright-eyed, tired, elated. Seeing them was proof the ascent is routinely done. Still I was apprehensive. They had performed in a high altitude world I had no actual knowledge of; perhaps it required skills and stamina beyond mine. I watched two climbers who were conversing in Italian. They stood at the base of the wall, in a jumble of ribbon-red rope. Describing their climb to an onlooker, gesturing as he spoke, one of the Italians lost his footing and fell back onto the snow. A fall right there is no more dangerous than slipping on a wet suburban lawn. But, still keyed up from the ascent, he screamed as though falling into the abyss.

The last Sunday morning of my stay I met Franzen in the square. The weather report promised fair conditions through the following afternoon, time enough for an ascent. He was to have asked the German lady to relinquish his services this once, since it was my final opportunity, and she had agreed. The climb was on. I went back to the hotel to get ready.

I laid out everything I thought I'd need and, on impulse, photographed the array. Clothing and gear covered the bed. In retrospect my gear and clothing were amateurish. Danner light-weight boots, fine for day hikes in New England but really inadequate for the Alps. Cotton long underwear. Blue jeans for climbing pants. Flimsy rental crampons that looked like those cheap roller skates kids had when I was a boy. But there was too much stuff and I would leave some things. My harness, for instance, still holding the earthy smell of Connecticut rock, and my helmet—I would do without them. Alphonse could tie me on without the harness, and he scoffed at the need for a helmet. But I would take up a pint of water that I'd brought from home. I fancied the idea of having some of my own deep-well water atop the famous Alp. If we didn't make the summit I would drink it at the Solvay Refuge, or the highest point we reached.

On the way to the hut that afternoon I stopped at Schwarzsee and sat for a few minutes, peeled an orange, and watched the tourists. This fellow wearing thick spectacles caught my attention. Gaunt and stoop-shouldered, around 55, he could have been typecast for a bookkeeper or school master but for his powder blue coveralls which looked wildly

implausible on him. Compared to my primitive trappings his outfit sug-
gested serious intentions, but I ruled him out as a Matterhorn contender,
deciding that the bib pants were an affectation.

Alphonse was already at the hut when I checked in. He ushered me
to a small room with bunk beds, advised me what to do in preparation
for morning, and urged me to relax. After I'd rearranged the contents of
my pack I took off my boots and stretched out on a cot. I felt set. Make
it or not, I had trained hard and would do my best. Such thoughts and
the wind whistling by the window behind my bed were calming. Later on
Alphonse looked in on me again, like a nervous mother, to make sure I
was resting. Subsequently there was a tap at the door.

"Come in!" In came the fellow with the state-of-the-art pants. His
bearing was tentative and apologetic. He spoke to me in German. "I'm
sorry, I don't understand German."

Hesitantly, as though he hadn't tried English in awhile, he asked if I
knew which cots were taken. I said I believed all of them were available.
He sat on the bunk diagonal to mine, meekly establishing it as his for the
night. We began a conversation that continued at the supper table, both
glad for someone to talk with. He had emigrated from Hungary to West
Germany a few years before and now lived in Berlin where he worked
as a chemist, an occupation that fit his bookish image. But I was wrong
to assume he wasn't aiming for the Matterhorn. Indeed he had come for
the climb, although he confessed to having been warned against it by the
instructor who'd tried him on the Rifflehorn.

I went to sleep between eight and nine, and was awakened by boister-
ous voices an hour or so later. By then the room was filled with people
and equipment. When I woke again I looked out the window to a clear
sky, bright moon and stars. We would go. I couldn't sleep anymore so got
up to use the privy, then went out in the yard and was surprised to see
lights on the mountain. The highest of them appeared to be a third of the
way up the ridge. It was only 3:20 a.m. A little after four Alphonse tied
me on and we climbed for about an hour with headlamps. Far beneath us
the village glowed, a picture for a Christmas card. "The lights of Zermatt,
what a sight," I remarked.

"Save your breath," he replied, all business now and going at it hard.

Farther along, still in darkness, we heard somebody above us yell "Rock!" In English. Alphonse jumped against the wall, hugging it like his high school sweetheart. Then he called for me to do the same. I pressed in against him, covering my head with my hands. In the next instant a shower of loose rock crashed on the ledge behind us. I hadn't fully realized at the time what an extremely dangerous moment that was. Alphonse hollered up, reprimanding the guy who'd kicked off the barrage. I didn't understand his harsh language but there was no mistaking his fury. I had to question the foolish decision not to wear a helmet.

An easy technical section called the Mosley Slab led to the Solvay Refuge, a crude hut smelling of urine. We went past it a short way before pausing for a break. We'd been out about two hours, which I knew and Alphonse said was excellent time. Now I felt sure we would do it.

Above the shoulder—a prominent feature of the Hörnli Ridge—we encountered patches of ice, and strapped on our crampons. I let him know I was wary of climbing on ice. "Oh, don't start crying now," said my taskmaster. The topmost pitches were more difficult although not so bad as that American climber we'd spoken with the year before had led us to believe. Endurance was key. For me it seemed like a tough final exam: if you'd prepared enough the actual test was almost anticlimactic. Across the long Swiss to Italian summit ridge was a well-trod furrow in the snow. Alphonse celebrated with a couple of *schlucks* from the bottle of schnapps he carried (something like drinking and driving, I thought—I was giddy enough with our success). I pushed some of my Connecticut deep-well water on him.

We were back in the lodge before noon. I paid Franzen and said farewell. He tried to get me to stay and rest awhile before leaving but, buoyed by having climbed the mighty Matterhorn, I still felt good and wanted to get going. I'd been there nearly three weeks preparing and climbing. I'd had enough of the place and my guide's regimentation.

Waiting on the crowded cable-car platform at Schwarzsee, I felt someone touch my arm. Still in his powder blues, the Hungarian-German shot me a weak smile. How had I done? He'd made it to the Solvay Refuge but there his guide had convinced him to give it up—their progress had been slow and the "really hard" part was yet to come. Better to have gone halfway than not at all, I thought, and told him so. Pleased with my own performance, it was easy for me to talk. Naturally he was sorely disappointed.

The next morning I caught the first train out of the valley. Before leaving Europe I wanted to see Lake Constance and cross it into Germany. It rained on and off, sometimes hard, most of the day. I had just made it. Few passengers boarded the train. I had a compartment of seats to myself, and read or gazed out the window as I pleased, interrupted only after certain stops, to show my rail pass. I traveled light, having shipped the climbing equipment and most of my clothes ahead to Kennedy. Like a Gypsy on the move I carried enough rolls, cheese, and chocolate to last me until night, if need be. Also tucked in my carryon bag was the lightweight camera I'd bought for the trip. On an unfinished roll it had a couple of latent images of Alphonse and me, grinning at the guy who'd offered to snap us on the top.

> "When I am on the wire I am alive. All else is waiting."
> (*Karl Wallenda—German-born American aerialist.*)

When I left Franzen and the Matterhorn in August 1985, I thought that was that. A satisfying adventure intended as a one-time kind of mid-life distraction. Now I could move on to more practical matters. So I thought then. But one thing leads to another.

Shortly after I returned home Bob Clark had a slide show of his trip to Zermatt. At that time he was part owner of a climbing shop where I went to ask a lot of questions about technical ascents, prior to my trip. Bob's stay in Zermatt coincided with mine and, just before my guided ascent he climbed the Matterhorn alone, soloed it his first time on the route, that is, *un-roped*, and doing his own route finding. This is all the more remarkable given that he knew two elite climbers from our home area who were involved in fatalities, heading up that Hörnli Ridge on their own.

One of Bob's slides, taken from the Italian side of the summit, captured the village of Cervinia showing through gaps in the clouds, as though seen from an airplane. That put another little bug in my head. I had invested all this time learning to climb and preparing for a serious mountain (by the end of my stay I was undoubtedly in the best shape of my life). Maybe before quitting this, I could climb the Matterhorn from Italy, where it is called *Il Cervino*.

That next summer I went up the Grand Teton, in Wyoming, with the Exum guides. And I did try the Italian ridge in 1987. But we were forced back at the Carrel Hut, a little more than halfway up the ridge, in the wee hours of the second day. Early that morning I was awakened by a flashlight in my face. The guide Enrico announced that the mountain was socked in and it was impossible to go up. His good news was that we could sleep in a while longer. But just minutes later lightning cracked viciously and thick wet snow was falling. The hut became a frenzied place, everyone wanted to escape at once.

In 1990, still driven by the Matterhorn, I tried the Italian ridge again, this time successfully, going with three Italians, a father and son—both Courmayeur mountain guides—and a physician-friend of theirs from Milan. Better equipped by then I was wearing heavy boots with wool socks and liners, but as we gained altitude above the hut my feet got so cold I thought I might not be able to continue. But then the sun came up, beautifully lighting Mount Blanc, to our backs as we climbed. The Italian ridge's difficult overhangs are fixed with ropes and cables to aid the climber. I wondered how the first men to ascend this side got past those brutal sections before they were rigged. We carried crampons (extra weight) all the way unnecessarily, the route entirely free of ice and snow that week. After we came down I found out that only one of my companions—the father, Cosimo—had ever been on the Matterhorn before, and he only once.

Now twenty-five years have passed since I first glimpsed the Matterhorn. My desire to climb a *real* mountain back in '84 seemed to me a natural outgrowth of all the long days I'd put in hiking Connecticut's hilliest northwest corner, and New York state's Catskill and Adirondack mountains. I didn't know much about the Matterhorn then, and had seized on it mainly for its reputation. By name it's probably the most recognized mountain in the world. Why it has such fame is unclear, unless you have seen it looming over the village of Zermatt. When the notion of climbing it first gripped me, in wishful moments I was fantasying its easiest, Swiss, route as a kind of mountain trail with blazes I might be able to follow on my own. When I actually saw the mountain and had spoken with Zermatt guides and climbers, I was a bit overwhelmed. I had no knowledge of rock climbing, and the monster sure looked forbidding.

As I've said, one thing leads to another. After I had learned enough for an ascent like the Matterhorn I kept climbing and improving until I was competent on rock routes that I considered difficult. I kept at it, I told myself, to stay prepped for other technical mountains I might do. I climbed in hiking boots. Since I wouldn't be using rock-climbing shoes in the mountains I didn't buy any for the first three years. Much of the time I'd go alone, with minimal gear, often climbing just one short route taking an hour or so after work, in winter coming out of the woods in the dark. Rock climbing was just a means to an end when I began but has long since become an obsessive pursuit in itself. By now I've no doubt frittered away as much time seeking out and climbing Connecticut crags as I did sitting in classrooms through eight years of grade school. Imagine that.

"...in mid-July 1926 Hitler left Munich with his entourage for a holiday on the Obersalzberg. He stayed in a secluded and beautiful spot situated high in the mountains on the Austrian border above Berchtesgaden, flanked by the Untersberg (where legend had it that Barbarossa lay sleeping), the Kneifelspitze, and the highest of them, the Watzmann. The scenery was breathtaking."

Ian Kershaw, *Hitler: 1889—1936 Hubris*

Sometimes you find a mountain; other times it finds you. We came to Berchtesgaden by train from Munich one autumn afternoon in the 1970s. Like a lot of Americans I was drawn to the place for its infamous past: Hitler's alpine refuge and the Nazi enclave had been situated on the adjacent Obersalzburg. Berchtesgaden's appeal is that of an ancient German village with steep paths, cobblestone alleyways, and a walled churchyard cemetery in the midst of the Bavarian Alps. The Watzmann, near the Austrian border, is the highest point around, and the highest mountain wholly within Germany. At 8900 feet it's not a giant but it's their

Matterhorn. After a few unsuccessful trips, I finally got to the loftiest of its three summits in 2003. It is one of several smaller mountains I've sought that don't require a guide for route finding or technical problems, and it can be done (optimistically) in a single long day's push.

The Middle Teton in Wyoming is another of those that can be done in one prolonged day. Mig Farina, Len Burns, and I were stormed off it on a final stretch near the top in 1996, but I went back in July 2004 with Aric Rindfleish, another climbing friend, and we made it to the summit. Coming down from the mountain, having started (and we would finish) in the dark, we walked out in a downpour. Late that night I stood for a long time in a hot shower trying to stop the uncontrollable shivers. My thought was *that's it*. No more. I'd had enough. I would still hike, and climb my familiar home rock routes as long as I could, but no more marathon days in the mountains.

I revisited Berchtesgaden in September '04 with Cathy and two of our friends. On a Sunday when they took off for Salzburg I hiked from the Königsee—a fiord-like lake—to the Watzmannhaus, a huge hiker's lodge just above the tree line. It's a little more than 4000 feet of elevation gain from the trailheads, a popular destination in itself, and the lodge enables an overnight stay for a fresh morning start for those after one or more of the Watzmann's three summits.

As I was having a snack on a bench outside the lodge an elderly gent sat next to me. We sat silently for a while until he opened with a question in German. When I explained my language handicap he switched easily to English in what sounded like a refined and rather pedantic British accent. Did I think it was going to storm? He had started up the mountain but had turned back because the upper reaches were in a cloud cover. Sudden storms are the bane of mountaineers. In one of our early Watzmann attempts Mig and I were halted at the start of the summit ridge by a developing thunderstorm. And on our first attempt of the Middle Teton, within just hundreds of feet of the top, I got a terrific shock—which knocked me down hard and sent my ice-ax flying (never to be recovered)—from a lightning strike at the summit. But on this day on the Watzmann, although visibility would be poor, it didn't look threatening.

This man was a playwright and professor of theater in Salzburg, about 12 miles north of Berchtesgaden. Belying his somewhat shaky, professorial appearance he was indeed an experienced climber. He and his *older* brother had done many ascents of Austria's Dachstein, and he said he'd been climbing the Watzmann annually for the past twenty-five years. Most impressive, he told me he had traversed its narrow, severely exposed summit ridge un-roped, and before it was protected with iron pegs and cables. But he maintained that he climbed with great care, said he valued life and wanted to live to be an old man. *(Old man?* He was 76 then!) It was an inspiring half-hour conversation. Seven years older than I and still hard at it.

On our return from that trip I had a letter from Mig, my enthusiastic hiking buddy for thirty years. He was suggesting we travel to easternmost Turkey the following year to climb Mount Ararat. It was tempting, but I declined. As I am now reaching the age more for reminiscing about the mountains than climbing them, I wish I had that one to retrace in my head, going up 17,000 foot Ararat and perhaps looking for remnants of the lost ark along the way.

Carlos Reyes

Ode to a Fossil Fern

The man who brings the ice
brings coal to our porch
in burlap bags but not today.
We could be those children
scrounging along the tracks
for bits of coal fallen from gondolas.
Our last piece of coal, I want to keep it,
with its delicate fossil of a fern exposed.
 My mother has no trouble
deciding between beauty or comfort in December.
In a room where you can see your breath
she breathes: *dust, dirt, black coal, fire...*
But fuel not fern is the final word
thrown on the dying fire where it begins to glow,
finely drawn pencil lines, finally taken to flame.
Yet I watch until my eyes burn,
all the heat I get, that and night's thin blanket.
Old clothes, coats the things
I would gladly trade to save the fern.

David Oestreich

Birthing Myths

As I sit now by the stones of the hearth,
the phoenix appears
so plainly inevitable. For if not
when lining the little nest of kindling
with soft tinder, or stepping back
as flames burst from between the twigs,
an endless flight of startled birds
(the smoke a shadow their brightness cast
upon the sky), or watching the glowing eggs
of embers slowly form—if not at these,
then surely when returning to find
the crumbling ash-gray down left
by departed fledglings; yes,
surely then, someone would have known
here was a story to tell.

Pseudotriton ruber

You have seen trees; many;
dozens of species. But the oak
at the park that took you and seven
of your childhood friends linked
hand in hand to span its trunk; and
the hickory, miles from any road,
which no one ever notices except
the squadron of bats hunkered

David Oestreich

in the shaggy hangars of its bark;
or the willow in your own yard,
that delicate giant wearing slim hearts
on each of its thousand sleeves—
is it not a sin to say, merely, these
are trees?
                    O surely we are fallen!
But let me strive for righteousness.
I will not say, *This afternoon*
I found a salamander. Rather
I will tell you of the drop of lava,
cool but moist, I found crawling in a rill
among the rocks, that I watched this
small, red leopard prowl the undergrowth
along the mossy corner of a log.
Fierce, shovel-headed Hades flame he was,
licking up millipedes and pill-bug eggs;
I left him there among the hemlocks
undisturbed, but you must know,
(by my poor tongue!) dear reader—
you must know
                    I've told you nothing.

George Looney

No Statues of Blind Poets

Tonight, in the hum of every street lamp,
the melody of the lost. Maladies
hang on beyond the dim, sour haloes
in which moths get drunk and poets' ghosts limp

on game legs gone bitter with the night. Damp,
grass seems to glow at the feet of statues
cemented to the center of town, lies
of generals and statesmen, not an imp

of a poet, blind in stone, among them.
The night's an orchestra and what it plays
isn't a music meant for anyone

a statue would be built of. Given time
and words enough, a blind poet's ghost sways
to night's music, absolving everyone.

George Looney

Ode to English Landscapes

Light over a field of rape, the clouds
precursors of something they can't name.

Such color requires more of us,
desire obstructing what's known.

In Turner's skies, lust would feel
at home. All that raw miasma
of color and light just to hold in air.

A shame, to think without Turner
no sky would've held such passion.

The world has nothing that comes close.

George Looney

The Hieroglyph of the Horizon

This gauze of air winds around
men and women who walk through it
and leave their likenesses.

The past must be like this,
all faint after-images and denial,

though memory won't keep a body
bandaged and whole and warm.

Grief is a hieroglyph scrawled inside
the body, its bird head
looking off to the horizon,

as if a rigid line could hold some solace
a body could breathe in and live off.

Donna Trump

Weight Shift

ELLEN WAITS AT THE WINDOW in the living room for her nephew, Jack, to come home from school. He walks from the bus with his head down, thick brown hair obscuring his face. Outside the porch, he checks the mail. No need, as Ellen is home during the day, but it is a habit that has been hard to break. Since the accident, she has lived here with him in this haunted house, flying off at night to work the graveyard shift at the hospital downtown. She likes to greet him when he gets home from school, although he doesn't seem to think much of the effort.

He sits with her, for a few minutes anyway, lured by the relentless hunger of a sixteen year-old boy. She and her sister never ate like this. It is almost pitiful, she thinks, how much he needs. Some days she can almost see the food transpose into new red muscle, an extra inch of bone, a squaring of brow and jaw. Ellen watches him now as he grabs another handful of cookies, peels open a bright yellow banana.

"How was school?" she says.

"Fine."

She knows not to expect more. "History test go okay?"

"Yup."

His fingers are long and thin, like her sister's were. There is a place below his eyes where sharp cheekbones suspend tight, smooth skin that could be a section of Jana's face. Ellen is reminded of a childhood game she and her sister played, where faces are compiled of thin strips, one across the forehead, one through the middle, one for the mouth and chin.

"Thanks for the snack. I still have a ton to do on my project," and he slides up the stairs to his room. He calls to her from the upstairs hallway: "I'm taking a pillow from Mom's bed."

"What is it you're working on, Jack?" She moves to the bottom of the stairs. "Can I see it?"

"It's not ready." She hears his door slam shut, and the click of the lock.

Jack was born the summer after Ellen graduated from high school. Ellen and Jana's father was long dead, and their mother's battle with alcoholism and lung cancer came to a close within weeks of Jana's discovery she was pregnant. Jack's biological father was a serious, scholarly type with such disregard for Jana he never bothered to put two and two together. The only father Jack would know—Jana's husband, Bill—was not scripted for nearly a decade.

That first day home after Jack was born, when she and Jana held him on the couch and he looked at them with creased forehead and dark, curious eyes, Ellen dismissed the life she had known. They slept with him in their mother's big bed for a week, until Ellen woke one night to find the sheets next to her twisted and damp, pillows scattered on the floor. Jana and Jack were gone. Running through the house, flipping on lights and calling for each of them, she found them in the basement. Jana had Jack swaddled in a blue receiving blanket, loaded into a laundry basket perched on top of the humming, empty dryer. Shhhh! Jana gestured wildly to her sister as she approached. Her eyes were empty with fatigue. He just fell asleep, she whispered. If you wake him, I'll kill you. Ellen returned to her room and her own bed. In spite of the July heat, the sheets were cool with disuse.

They split everything down the middle: the life insurance money, the house, the hours to care for Jack. Jana took midnight to noon, Ellen noon to midnight. It wasn't fair to let the baby sleep through a whole shift, leaving him wakeful and fretting for the other sister. They passed him off like a baton in a relay, running off to the grocery store, a college class, part-time work. He seemed none the worse for it.

When Jack turned two, Jana bought the canoe. "What do you think, Jack?" she asked him, waking him up from his nap that July afternoon, against Ellen's protests.

"No one in her right mind wakes a sleeping baby," Ellen said. "I can't get one thing done around here when he's awake."

"Dirt keeps, little sister. I want to show him our next adventure." The baby rubbed his eye with one fisted hand, laid the other hand gently across Jana's breast, like a promise.

"Boat," he said.

"Yes, you smart boy, it's a boat. And you and Mama are going to learn how to swim."

"Do whatever you want, Jana. Just make sure *you* pay for the damn thing, and that includes the lessons."

But Jana didn't seem to hear. She was tucking the baby into the car seat, pulling the safety strap over his head. Then she drove away from the curb, the thwarts and seats and guts of the canoe shining through its sheer yellow skin like seeds and membranes inside a section of lemon.

When Jana and Bill's private plane went down on a frigid day in January, Ellen moved herself back into the home in which she and Jack, in turn, grew up. The house itself was markedly different: roof raised to accommodate a bedroom for Natalie and Eva, Bill's young daughters; walls bumped out on the main floor yielding to a spacious, updated kitchen; basement transformed from moldy concrete blocks to a sleek studio for Jack. Still, in its grip, Ellen felt squeezed into the person she was the last time she lived here, the summer Jack turned five. The one who'd grown tired of overdue bills, dirty laundry piled to the rafters. The one who'd grown sick of Jana's steady stream of sleep-over boyfriends, with Jack right down the hall.

Weeks after the crash, on an evening in March, Ellen and Jack cleared two feet of wet snow off the narrow crescent-shaped driveway and walkways surrounding the house. Snow sparkled like mica in the light of the streetlamps.

"You could have a heart attack moving this stuff," she said, out of breath, arms folded over the handle of the shovel. She took off her hat, and opened her coat.

"Are we the *only* ones on the block without a snow blower?" Jack stopped, cocked an ear dramatically toward the buzzing motors up and down the street. "Do you hear that noise, Aunt Ellen? That's the sound of modern technology."

"This used to be your Mom's and my job," she ventured. "When we were your age. Shoveling snow."

"Five degrees warmer and it'd be rain," Jack said. The plastic scoop of the shovel shuddered and twisted on the wooden handle with each load of snow he threw over his shoulder. He had stripped down to only his jeans and a sweater, sleeves pushed up. His heavy parka, gloves and hat were strewn across a snow bank. Sweat steamed off his shoulders and head.

"We had rules," she said. "Jana hated doing the driveway, so her job was the sidewalk, the front walk, and the steps. When she was done, she had to go inside and make hot chocolate while I finished up."

When he walked by on the next pass, he paused in front of her. The backs of his hands were flecked with tiny dots of paint. Plaster, like white, chalky dirt, caked his finger nails, lightened some of the hairs of his eyebrows. Underneath, his eyes were dark coves in his narrow, angular face. She worried he didn't sleep. Often when she left for the hospital he was already sequestered in the basement, saw whining, hammer pounding. She imagined him working through the night, disrupted only by the thin light of morning slipping through the room's small transom windows.

"She made good hot chocolate," he said. He handed her the shovel and went in the house. Ellen looked up to the street light, saw the snow had started again. She took both shovels to the garage. Under cover, she watched snow falling from the sky meet snow swirling up from drifts, until, even with gloves, she could no longer feel her fingertips.

The divide and conquer system failed early in Ellen's third year of nursing school, when she had to report to the hospital at irregular hours for clinical rotations. "I don't see how I'll be able to work and take care of Jack *and* finish my degree," she said to Jana. Jack was napping, and would be down for three hours at least, having fallen asleep in the car after his

"Mommy and Me" swimming lessons at the Y. Across the table, Jana's eyes were bloodshot and swollen. Her blond hair was green.

"Which would you rather do?" Jana asked, raking her hand through hair clotted and snarled with chemicals. The kitchen smelled like a pool.

Ellen started to speak, paused, started again. "It's not that easy, Jana."

"Well, I know what I want. I'd rather take care of Jack."

"Convenient, sis, except if I were to leave. And then, for God's sake, how would you eat?"

Jana looked down at the table. "And just where," she said, almost in a whisper, "would you go?"

Ellen stared at the top of her sister's head, shifted her gaze as Jana looked up.

"I'm sorry if it's not what you wanted," Jana said. "But I think we might be alright now, Jack and me, on our own."

"Right." Ellen threw off her shoes and hauled herself over to the daybed on the porch. Mid-September cool washed through the screens. Downed leaves crunched and skittered on the street outside, releasing the last of their loamy smell. Soon the screens would have to come down, the storm windows up, leaves raked, snow shoveled. Ellen saw chores line up in front of her like cars in a traffic jam. She closed her eyes, but did not sleep.

Ellen stands in front of the entry way closet, boots and coats, hats and mittens, ski helmets and an ancient set of sleigh bells, tarnished metal globes on a long, thin strip of weathered leather, in disarray at her feet. Natalie and Eva's pink and purple winter coats, she thinks, can be given away. Ellen will keep Jana's clothing, although it fits her more in size than style, and Jack is already almost big enough to wear what Bill left behind. She checks her watch: nearly five. Time to wrap this up, make some decisions about what will go. Dinner at six, another chance to worm her way into Jack's brain, decode his words, decipher his emotions. She will leave for work at ten.

The sleigh bells shiver as Jack stomps by her. His arms are loaded with dented, color-swathed paint cans, their delicate wire handles decorating his forearms like so many bangle bracelets. The cans bump against each other with dull sloshes and thuds.

"Where'd you get all those?" she asks him, as he flies by, heading for the basement.

"Hazardous waste center."

Other peoples' cast-offs. It feels like a revolving door—she trying to bring some order into this space they now share, he sneaking in more crap, right behind her. It's more than the paint. It's the plywood scraps, half-full buckets of plaster, pieces of two-by-four, chicken wire. "What do you need it all for?" she shouts after him, but he is already in the basement. He hasn't heard the question.

There are things she regrets, for him. No father, two crazy mothers, a step-father with two built-in little sisters, now only one ineffective aunt. Still, sometimes it feels as though she will be crushed by the weight of it all—this dumpsite collection of construction material leftovers, the awkward silences in what passes for their conversations, the maddening, fearsome way he looks at her, the hooded gaze that reminds her this is not the life he expected.

There was the day she arrived home to find two police cars parked in front of the house. A few neighbors—older people who had known their parents, younger ones with small children—gathered, whispering, at the chain link fences on either side of their lot. Ellen kept her eyes on the ground as she walked past them, stepping carefully over Jack's small bike abandoned on the sidewalk.

Inside, she found Jana and three blue-uniformed police officers. The officers all stood, towering over her sister as she sat in the old wing-back chair in the living room. The mess—the sheer chaos—of the room struck Ellen as if she were seeing it for the first time: unwashed dishes on the end tables; a sippy cup leaking apple juice into the carpet; scores of colorful plastic figures splayed over the floor. Jack was sending toy cars down a three-foot long slide, shrieking with delight as they crashed at the bottom.

"Jana, what's going on?"

The story was that a neighbor had seen Jana leaving the house on more than one occasion, in the afternoon, while Jack was asleep. How did this neighbor know the baby was in the house? Ellen asked. She came in today to investigate, one officer said. The doors were unlocked? Jana shrugged, face pale as sand.

Child Protective Services would be contacting them. No, it was unlikely the baby would be removed from the home. This time. But don't leave your kid home alone anymore, ma'am. Not even for a minute. You would not believe, the female officer said, cap in hand, what I have seen happen. The police officers let themselves out.

Jana perched at the edge of the chair. Ellen could see her breaths were shallow and rapid. Her eyes were fixed on Jack. Ellen cleared a space off the sofa and sat. "What in God's name were you thinking, Jana?"

Jana covered her face with her hands.

"You don't deserve him," said Ellen.

Then the sobs began, inhuman gasps and moans, sending Jack into his own spate of tears on the opposite side of the room. "Baby, come here," Jana said, arms open. He ran to her and she gathered him into her lap. Jana kissed his head, tucked him under her chin.

"I left him for about fifteen minutes. Two, maybe three times." Jana shook her head. Jack stuck his thumb in his mouth, rubbed the length of his mother's arm with one chubby hand. "It won't happen again."

"You—"

"Wait a minute, Ellen. I'm not done. I may not deserve him. You may be right about that. But," she said, voice unsteady, "he *is*, by the grace of some incredibly benevolent and forgiving God, mine. Whether I deserve him or not."

It was the first time Ellen saw their futures as separate, a highway ending in a red and white striped barricade, with detour arrows to the left and right.

Ellen arrives at the hospital just before the shift starts. Her patients on the rehab floor are survivors, people who, by all rights and expectations, should be dead. The recently retired man whose neck was crushed by a falling branch as he cleared trees in his yard on a summer evening. Now he sits in a wheelchair and can't use his hands. The woman who fell off a stepstool while changing a light bulb, smacked her head in exactly the wrong spot, was comatose for months. Now she looks out from expressionless eyes to a world she may or may not see. The boy who drove his car to school while he was high. Now he walks with long, metal braces and long, metal canes, and his back is scarred like the roadmap he'd like to be reading, anywhere but here. She scans the notes of their daily activities, their struggles with strength, balance, shifting weight from hand to hand, hip to hip. They sleep now, dreaming, she imagines, of dexterous fingers and toes, laughter, and second chances. In the morning, she will help them bathe and poop and pee and dress, reminding them that progress must be measured in small intervals. When she leaves for her sister's house, she will forget everything she has told them.

On the drive back, she sees a small plane shining against the colors of the sunrise. Natalie and Eva were with their father and Jana in the plane. Ellen and Jack had been invited, but neither was fond of flying. Jack had once told his mother he might like it more if parachutes were equipped with mechanical wings instead of just a mushroom of air to break a fall. But for Jana, it had been the next adventure. Bill, the flying instructor, became Bill, the boyfriend, the fiancé, the husband, the father. He took Jack to the Boundary Waters, where they canoed and fished and hiked and traveled light.

Ellen thinks it must have been something about the air that day: bitter cold, still as stone. Wasn't cold air heavy and dense? How could they have hoped to stay up there, with so little lift beneath them? And then it was just her and Jack, rattling around in that overloaded house. By the grace of a benevolent and forgiving God, she and Jack, unlikely survivors.

She had left him because of the business. Jana had been taking classes at the technical college and started her own company. She left the baby on a few desperate occasions when she needed to make a naptime delivery: to the daddy at work on his birthday, the grandma in the hospital, the angry girlfriend. Jana hired a babysitter after the incident with the police, delaying her days of profit by another several months. But the business was operating in the black by the time Jack was three. In the fall of that year, Jana enrolled him in preschool, and Ellen, for the first time, felt as though she were dragging the two of them down, instead of the other way around.

Ellen knew nothing of her sister's work until months after the police visit. It seems Jana had seen the advertising potential in the crowds at Lake Harriet. Ellen was on a rare date—Eric was his name, another student nurse. Running down the hill to the lake's west side, Ellen stopped short, yanking Eric's arm as he flew by. Framed against the backdrop of the delicate gables and spires of a band shell, a woman and a small boy in bright orange life jackets paddled a nearly transparent canoe. In bold lettering, across the sides and just underneath the gunwales, were the words: "JJ's Air Blooms," and a telephone number. Tethered by shiny ribbons to the front and back thwarts were two gigantic bouquets of balloons: colorful latex spheres interspersed with glittering Mylar in the shapes of roses, irises and daisies. The balloons bobbed and danced high above the wake of the gliding canoe.

"Isn't that your phone number?" said Eric.

"It's my sister," said Ellen.

"Who's the kid?"

Ellen didn't answer. At that moment, there was nothing in the world but the yellow sun piercing the canoe, and her sister, flying without wings across the smooth, dark surface of the lake.

A month before school is out for the summer, she hears hollow booms in the garage, interspersed with Jack's curses and moans. She finds Jack with two hands overhead supporting the canoe, the back half of which is still suspended by ropes to the garage ceiling. She realizes, with some satisfaction, he has few options but to accept her help. Once the canoe is on the cement floor, Jack and Ellen pick it up by the thwarts and carry it out to Jana's car, parked in the driveway. "It's lighter than I thought," says Ellen.

"Wait," he says. "I want to do this by myself, like Mom used to." Ellen lets go of the canoe. Jack flips it over, lifts the bow, sidles himself underneath until his head and shoulders disappear. Ellen sees his hands come out to grasp the gunwales. He raises the canoe's center thwart onto his narrow shoulders, the canoe tipping up and down like a see-saw. Jack takes small, steady steps toward the back of the car.

"How can you see where you're going?" Ellen says.

Jack raises the canoe to the roof of the car. As he slides it forward, it screeches and bangs in rumbling protest, but soon it is centered. He ducks out from under the stern and beams at his aunt.

"Wasn't so bad," he says.

"You did great," she says.

"Come on. We have to tie it down."

When they are done, she asks him where he is going. Hot date on Lake Harriet?

Jack shrugs, gives her a sheepish grin. He reminds her the art show is next week. Wouldn't miss it for the world, she says. And he is off.

For a few years she didn't see him much more frequently than at holidays and special occasions, from the time she moved to her own apartment until the summer Jack was nine. At his birthday party that July, Jana invited Ellen to join them at the beach the next day. There, without preamble or explanation, she asked if Ellen would consider taking Jack one weekend a month.

"Is everything alright, Jana?" Ellen asked. Jana slouched against the webbing of a lawn chair, toes digging into coarse, dirty sand. Ellen sat cross-legged on a blanket, back straight and neck craning, squinted eyes raking the nearly uninterrupted mass of children's bodies in the lake.

"Don't do it if you don't want to."

"I didn't say I didn't want to." She shot to her feet. "Where's Jack? Do you see him? I told him not to go out too far, but now I can't see him anywhere."

"You know what? Just forget it, Ellen. You'll turn him into a godforsaken basket case."

A blonde and deeply tanned lifeguard had ascended the stand and blew her whistle with alarming insistence. She lifted her arms like a priest at Mass, in odd contrast to the urgent blasts of the whistle. "What in God's name is she doing?" Ellen hopped from foot to foot, peering out to the water, jiggling her arms as if to shake out the fear. "Jana, I think you'd better go in to get him."

"Boo!" he said, hands reaching from behind Jana's head to blindfold her. Jana peeled Jack's blue-tinged, wrinkled fingers from her face. "Come here, you!" she said. "Give your Auntie a hug. You're making her nuts."

He threw his arms around Ellen and she held him until the panic bled out of her fingers and toes. His head nearly reached her chin. Ellen rubbed her face in his wet hair, opened her eyes to see crystals of sand like tiny jewels against his pink scalp. "Your mom says you can stay over with me next weekend," she said, still holding him tight. "What do you think of that?"

Jack mumbled into her shirt, but she heard the question, clear as day: Why'd you move out, Aunt Ellen? If she knew then what she knew now, she might have told him. How she woke up one morning in that crazy, free-form life of her sister's and felt absolutely without weight, an oddity, a reprieve. Insubstantial. Unnecessary. How if he were hers, she would have handled it all differently, and better. It would have offended him, for his mother's sake if not his own, and she would, eventually, take every word of it back. But the opportunity passed, and she whispered, instead, into his cold, damp ear: How about the zoo?

It is the morning of the art show, and he is eating again. Second breakfast or early lunch, she's not sure. He is hunched over his food like he must defend it against the competition. There is the current issue of *3-D Art* beside him on the new granite countertop, but he hasn't looked at it. At last glance, he was reading the back of the cereal box. Now when she looks up from mopping the kitchen floor, she sees him watching her, shaking his head.

"She was right about you," Jack says.

Oh, Lord, she thinks. Here it comes. "How so?"

"She said you'd be cleaning at your own funeral."

Ellen sees an opening. "Well," she says, "what would your mother be doing, right now, if she were here?" She places the mop in the bucket, rests the long wooden handle against the sink. She comes around the counter and climbs up on a wood and leather stool.

"Forget it," he says, opening the magazine.

"No, really. I'd like to know."

He flips through the pages, as if looking for his place. Ellen waits. "She had this thing about how people shouldn't eat alone," he says, nose still in the magazine. He has stopped on a two-page glossy advertisement for clay, plaster and odd-looking tools.

"What do you mean?"

"She'd always sit with me, whenever I ate." This time he looks at her.

Ellen almost says, "That's quite a commitment," but holds her tongue. Instead, she imagines her sister, here with them now, keeping them company as Jack eats.

He goes back to inhaling the cereal. When he finishes the second bowl, he clears his dishes. "This sucks for you, doesn't it, Aunt Ellen?" he says, loading the dishwasher. "If I was just a few years older, you wouldn't even have to be here."

Ellen leans toward him, across the cold granite. "I have nothing," she says, "believe me, *nothing*, better to do, Jack."

He turns his head to her, quick as a wish. "She used to say the exact same thing."

It was about three years ago that the apologies started. A message on a Tuesday or Wednesday, Jack's guilty voice explaining how Bill had some free time this weekend, maybe they would all—his little sisters, too—go canoe camping on the river, he knows she hates camping, does she mind? Then the cancellations later in the week, can you find another person to take to the game, the Children's Theater, the special exhibit at the museum, Aunt Ellen? And finally, the phone call at one in the morning on a crisp October night. Heart racing, she fumbled the handset, nearly dropping it to the bedroom floor.

"Did I wake you?"

"What's up, Jana?"

"I need to tell you something."

"You're scaring me."

"No. It's not like that. It's about Jack."

"What's wrong with Jack? Is he in trouble?"

"No, no. He just doesn't…he told me he doesn't want to do the weekend thing with you anymore. He'd rather sleep late, hang out with his friends. It's what he told me."

Ellen sat at the edge of her bed, straightened her sleep-messed hair in the dark mirror over the dresser.

"Ellen, are you there?"

"Yes," she said. "I'm here."

She enters the school on a hot night in June. Peonies planted at the entrance lean over with the weight of sweetly scented blooms. The air inside is artificially cool and smells of ancient floor wax, paint and unwashed clothing. Ahead, in the lobby, a crowd has gathered around a piece of artwork. Students and adults stand two and three deep, but the sculpture towers over them. From here she sees the canoe, suspended, somehow, above the heads of even the tallest in the group.

She moves closer, close enough to see the figures inside the canoe: solid, three-dimensional sculptures of Jana and Bill, Natalie and Eva. The girls each hold a paddle, pointed out to the side, at a ninety degree angle to the canoe. Along the heavily painted aft edge of each paddle there is a line, like keys on a piano, of delicate white feathers. They are attached so they flutter with every passing movement of air. Although all the figures, and the canoe itself, are obscured in layer upon layer of pastel-shaded paint, the likenesses to the subjects are remarkable.

In spite of herself, Ellen looks for her own image in the sculpture. She has made her way through the strata of viewers so that nothing stands between her and the statue. She takes in the figure of the boy who, like Atlas, suspends the canoe, overhead, on thickly muscled arms and torso. His back is straight, but his knees are bent with the weight of it.

She cannot find herself. She is not a part of the piece.

Ellen steps closer, then thinks she may have to step back to see. Removing herself from the crowd, she spots it: a hand, like skin over bone, layered on the back of Jana's hand. Same left and right, with nearly camouflaged arms along the backs of Jana's arms, and a waif of a torso, pasted onto Jana's back. Still stepping back, Ellen sees the head, with a face so much like her own she must blink back tears. Tucked behind Jana's mane of hair, and with half her features pressed up against her sister's slender neck, Ellen's expression is nearly hidden. Her one eye is closed. She wears half a Mona Lisa smile.

Ellen has stepped back so far, she leans against the cool glass of the door through which she entered. She hears Jack's voice, spots him among students who have just arrived. A girl with pink hair lifts her long, ballet-dancer's arms to his chest, straightens the tie Jack wears with his T-shirt and khaki shorts. Other kids form a tight ring around him. His sharp-edged face is a diamond of light. In just a minute, Ellen thinks, she will go and stand with them, in the circle. She will tell her nephew what a beautiful piece he has created, what a fine, strong man he is becoming. Yes, she will do this, and more, in a moment. Until then, she will rest here, smell the sweet skin of her sister's neck, and feel the pulse of her sister's strength, right next to her own.

A. D. Winans

The Demise of Jazz in North Beach

no cool cats in North Beach anymore
no cool cats blowing the horn
no jazz at the old Purple Onion
nobe-bop snapping fingers
no fallen angels spreading their legs
on the way home after a conversation
with God
no black cats improvising the blues
no white dudes riding the midnight express
no stoned soul train musicians blowing
mean clean notes crucified suffocating
in the smoking mirror of their minds
gone buried in the decadence
of collective madness

Nick Ripatrazone

Oklahoma in Ten Minutes

1
The one-room courthouse and the overgrown
creosote and the window the shape of a door
and the pickup's tracks settled in maroon mud.

2
Jenny and her baskets: crosslets woven red
and white, both colors bleached and bled, but
you can't blame her for that; the stitching
is tight and clean. Her earrings are longer
than her hair, tucked behind full ears, looped
back under her chin.

3
I've never been in a saloon, but you have,
standing at one end of the bar, five of them
at the other, hands on belts like they were palming
revolvers, buckles like sex. Wood there
was old and varnished, auburn but pale
in parts, like skin.

4
You had to smoke so we stopped, idling
in so much heat, hot from your mouth,
blowing up into wind I could not feel.
I left you and walked behind the red trailer
and spit in the grill's ash. I found a purple
and white dress crumpled in the switchgrass.
It was a four, your mother's size.

5
Your Dodge has more rust than blue but God
the paint that remains cools my palms while
I wait for you, inside with that cashier, college
across her low chest, eyes speaking light
words. I hope she knows what she will never
get but I could be wrong; Lord knows

6
that Happiness is Being Indian,
as the sticker says above the gas cap.
You sleep with your glasses on
but they never break (I am all over the place,
limbs on limbs, but you are solid and cold, and

7
you hate it when I call you chief
even though we share the same blood).

8
I never believed you about Bill Pickett
until your brother showed me that 16mm
reeling across the pocked concrete walls,
how Bill kissed the bull to bring it down,
falling while keeping his mouth
on its mouth, arms heavenward.
I laughed and you hated that I laughed,
kept on with your Hot Damn shots,
cinnamon lips worse than salt
and said you were going to the bathroom

9
but left, went outside, hiked
the paddock and rustled the cows
awake, but I stopped you

10
and that decision will stay in your mind.
In four years not a single moment
forgotten, good or bad. I should
be thankful for that, for your thighs
and the crease of your nose, your
able hands nearly black, but I
am not thankful. I want to leave.

Oars

My father found the canoe far from water:
an hour's walk, at a steady pace, from Keilen Pond
or even the weak stream that curled parallel
to the red trail. You need a foot of water
for this, he said, but I knew that wasn't true,
not untrue maybe, but false. You can drown
in an inch so you can float in the same.
After brushing away branches he found
two cases of Old Milwaukee, drained
but returned to the cardboard cases. So we
had bottles but no beer. Cases but no oars.
And not even a drop of water to stay afloat.

Nick Ripatrazone

Ann

In 1961 my mother stopped reading
books, magazines, pamphlets pinned
beneath windshield wipers, fliers
stuffed in mailboxes, letters written
longhand or typed. She would not
receive anything printed or transcribed,
so I had to read everything, delivered
in an even monotone, thumbs up
to note the end of a paragraph.
I thought structure had significance,
but she was sold on content and context,
and when I repeated words she savored
the sounds like good caramel.
People asked me how she got by, how
anybody could unlearn words; I said
she saw the red of a stop sign
and ignored the white, the blue
of half-priced peaches, green
grass bleached yellow at noon.
You only need words for words.
They are not the end of all things.

Nick Ripatrazone

Mildew, Minnesota.

After Theodore Roethke

It could have been the breeze
that tongued through the cracked glass,
spooling and spinning, feathered chervil
fluttering like paused breaths, the boot-
stomped shit curdled between floor
boards, yellow feed pressed against cedar;
or the faint life light wambling in parallel,
pulsing rows that allowed saltwort to grow
in a Blaine cellar, dead as duff.

Brent Fisk

Blizzard of '78

The snow swirled and eddied on its own
picket line, slowed the factory in ways the strike
never could. My father worked the clock
like an aching knuckle, lunch pail as pillow, fitful
dreams for sheets. His mistress, a hot shower.

My brother and I hollowed out
the piles of snow, ate soup boiled on a camping stove,
pierced the darkness with a badgered light,
giggles tethered to wrinkle-skinned restlessness.

Our mother disowned us
when she slept, hard-boiled and deep,
steeping like tea, or dyed eggs in vinegar.
We howled with the wind and rattled
the basement's cinder block walls

Too much of anything will take on the itch
of wool. Another day and we'd have split
our skin, become some feral other.
Chinese torture of slow thaw, the tick tock
of a dripping gutter. I wolfed down whole sandwiches
of ice and air. My father fed
ore into the ovens, played nice
for the foreman, doubling
the blinds on the quarter hour
he came home rich with matchsticks but poorer for it:
They cut his shifts to rags like dirty shirts.

My brother and I took up our hammers
struck at the frozen floor of the flooded garage.
Our father parked the station wagon on the street,
came up silent with a snow shovel cradled in his busted hands.
He helped remove what we'd cracked and broken.
Mother floated behind the washed out curtains,
bright as a green spring leaf but less certain.

CB Follett

Dream Water Boy

*With a tip of the watering can
to Eduardo Galeano*

I'm fond of the Dream Water Boy,
his watering can of burnished silver,
hid quick shortened steps as he edges between
rows of lettuce, each head singing its part.
They glory in Adestes Fideles, except for the
tenor who has wilted in hot sun.

The Dream Water Boy has errands
but spares a spritz of water for the tenor romaine,
which straightens on middle C
and refreshed, sings ahead of the the others
to an early finish.

Chilies click nearby on their stems,
giving a samba beat and the Dream Water Boy
begins to cha cha cha across the lawn spilling
precious dream-drops as he goes.

One falls on the quick brown fox who licks
his snout at the scent of chicken in the pot.
Another falls on the chicken who squawks
at a sky full of sharpened teeth.

*Come here, DreamWater Boy, before
there is nothing left in your watering can.*

I am in need of dreams and you are spilling
them like seeds and we know
the water in the bottom holds the sludge
of nightmares.

Last time, my nimble Dreamkin, you
squandered the top water on three frogs and a spider.
By the time you got to me, dragons and
hagfish jumbled out, all gaping mouths
and fiery breath.

It was all I could do to hold them off,
insisting they had important archtypes to discuss.
"It's summer," I persisted, "archtypes do not
appear until winter, or at the least, fall."
I need dreams that frolic and contain pastel.
I want to swim in Aegean waters
with sirens and mermaids.

The Dream Water Boy is flagging, his shoulder
droops and the can dips. If I hurry
perhaps I can slide under
the spillage, and I pick up my barberpole legs
and begin to *ponk ponk* in his direction.

As I launch myself over slippery grass,
the spray changes to rust. Scaly fingers
poke out the sprinkler holes and bat wings
rise over the opening. Too late. Nightmare water
pours, gurgling and spitting, and I
slide, my body hot with this mistake,
dig my fingers into dirt;
I need brakes, but the ground is wet as ooze,
just the thing for bog creatures
and maddened toadfish.

CB Follett

Stop pouring, Dream Water Boy.
Pick up the spout.
Oh I am doused
with a night of dark wings and warts.

Je Ne Sais Quoi

Arranging paper for what we are now,
we move along the path
of irreducible stains
that loosen the teeth
of the way we want to be
so that slipstreams
of our most carefully woven connections
refuse to turn to the left,
as we instruct
virgins in perfect hospital corners
that lead them to impress their scent
on a man lurking around every corner,
separate from each other
though the errand is the same for them all, for us
with our loose fingers, our four chambered
heart that thumps with a jazzed beat or a
Marley clash of notes rising
out of the Jamaican night with the smoke
and the sweet smell of music untrammeled
by the scrim of correct thinking and how the dogs
wag by the shore and pass their thick tongues
over the window sill where the pie cooled yesterday
and the yellow bird sings
Aida in the hot buggy night
that is submerged
in a fat smell of gardenias.

outside, calling

a cairn of stones
blue flies cracking through sunlight

raven with its jagged call
and rivers green as avocado

no one asked us

rub an egg against my skin
to absorb my restlessness

heavy copper coins
blackbirds that visit in my dreams

three souls, we have, that linger
for a few days working on transition

the great cordilleras pound south
harboring ghosts that whisper

I eat flint corn, brush my hair
with fir needles

a stone falls into the cool water
and a flower blooms up and fades

sparrows splash in a puddle,
stamping their fragile tines

a white casing flutters
like a concertina dried now,

CB Follett

and thinned by wind, each loop
rattles with infinitesimal whelks

and like a lithe moccasin
the river showing its white

throat over and over
winds down the Sierra descent

ever flicking its forked tongue
for a taste of the sea

Denton Loving

Casting Out

M Y BROTHER JAY'S TROUBLES had started the previous
Saturday with a force of straight line winds that left a two-day
trail from Texas to Tennessee. All over Powell Valley, trees of every size
had been blown sideways. Giant roots as thick as a man had been ripped
apart like strips of licorice. Grace Bailey's trailer was moved two inches
off its foundation, and every sheet of tin on Mack Jones' barn was yanked
up, nail by nail, blown across the Back Valley Road and scattered over his
hay field. Two barns and the skeleton of an old house were knocked down
completely on Straight Creek.

On Sunday morning, when the torrents of rain were soaked into the
earth and the high winds were replaced with a gentle breeze, Jay and I
walked through the woods surveying the damage and finding most of the
fallen trees had not torn down any fences. There were only a few places
where branches lay against the barbed wire or metal clips had broken
away from the fence posts. Those were easy problems to fix.

The roots of some trees were knocked loose, allowing them to sway in
the remaining winds. They creaked, giving me an eerie feeling. The noise
was like a warning to the others trees in the woods that one of their own
was on his last legs.

Jay had looked at every fallen tree, measuring in his head how tall each
had been, as well as how big around. He considered what kind of trees
had fallen—pines, oaks and sassafras—and he guessed at their ages.

"That storm didn't do us no favors," Jay said. The leaves were soft
with the rain, less noisy than usual.

"It won't take us long to clean up," I said, trying to cheer him.

By this time, we had walked to the back side of the farm, along the fence line that separated our woods from the back of Aunt Vonda's yard. Daddy owned the woods on every side of Vonda except for the front side that faced Tranquility Lane. She had chosen the name for the little road, which we joked was anything but tranquil since Vonda lived there. Daddy used to own Vonda's property too until she guilted him into selling her a piece of land so she could come back to Tennessee from Ohio. He knew it was a mistake then, and we've all regretted it ever since. The fence surrounding her land, six strands of barbed wire instead of the usual four or five, was more to keep us out than to keep the cows in.

At Vonda's house, the winds had all but pulled up a white poplar that had grown more sideways than should have been allowed. While the loosened roots were on our side of the fence, the majority of the tree hung over Vonda's side. Now that its roots were weakened, it leaned even more. The tree gave off a death rattle as its furrowed bark rubbed and pushed against the tightly stretched strands of barbed wire.

Long before Saturday evening's wind storms, Daddy had gone twice to cut that tree down, and both times Vonda had chased him off. Daddy wasn't exactly afraid of Vonda, but he didn't like to get in the middle of any trouble with her either.

That afternoon, all Jay said was, "I'll have to figure later on some way to deal with that mess."

Without telling Daddy or me, Jay parked his truck on Tranquility Lane the next morning and went to cut down that tree. Daddy was loafing at the Co-op as he did every Monday morning. And Vonda was on her daily run to the Wal-Mart in Middlesboro.

With one slanted cut from his camouflage-colored chain saw, the tree's top end made its journey to the ground with a loud but dull thud and the rustle of limbs and leaves. Released from its burden, what was left of the trunk jerked back and upright as if the ground had reclaimed what had unintentionally been given away. He made quick work of stripping the poplar of its limbs. Then he threw the debris across the fence as fast as he could until there was nothing left on Vonda's side but the tree's long, straight trunk lying like a fallen soldier on the battlefield.

He only stopped when he needed to catch his breath, but Vonda returned before he could have the job finished. Now, I never believed what she said about having second sight, but Jay said she came ripping past her "Jesus Loves You" sign and into her driveway like she already knew he was there. He could see her cussing before he could hear her, even before she could get out of her little red Sunfire that looked too sporty for her seventy-odd years.

Vonda was a little brown paper sack of a woman, full of nothing but bones and spite. She wore a faded red sweatshirt with the hood tight around her head that hid most of her face, but Jay could see she was angry, down right pissed off. More mad than he had ever seen her.

"Hell and damnation boy. I'll have your hide and hang it on that fence to dry. I'll slice you straight up the middle like the dirty snake you are," she said. "You rotten heathen. Cutting down my tree as soon as I turn my back."

Jay started to cross through the strands of barbed wire as if standing on the other side would protect him. But Vonda's streak of words seemed to make those six tight strands of wire attack him. His shirt caught on the sharp metal and tore. His hands were scratched and bloody before he realized he couldn't get through the fence. By that time, Vonda was getting closer. She was breathing hard from the constant yelling and the slight incline from her driveway.

"How are you going to put that tree back?" she said between huffs. "I want it back just the way it was."

Vonda never was accused of being the most rational person.

"There ain't no putting it back," he said. "I'm sorry, but it had to be done."

"I'll say what has to be done around here."

"Now, you hold on," Jay said. "That tree was on our side of the fence, and it was damaged. I did you a favor by cutting it down before it tore the fence down."

"Boy, you're gonna split hell wide open with that mouth."

"I was trying to clear it so you wouldn't have a mess in your yard. But if you don't quit your damn fussing, I'll leave."

"Don't you talk rough to me boy," she said, as if Jay's foul mouth had given her renewed spirit. "Don't you get in my face. I'll flat take you down. You'll come back a ragged piece of meat. I'm gonna get my gun, and we'll see who's fussing then."

She wobbled down the hill like a crow that won't fly, and then she turned back to face Jay again. "You'll be sorry you cut down that tree. I'll see the rot inside you come out before I'm done." And then she continued climbing up her steps to fetch her gun.

As wild as Vonda is, it's unlikely she would have actually shot Jay. Even if she had fired, chances are good she would have missed. She once tried to shoot a garden snake, but, aiming several feet too high, she shot through her window and took out her microwave instead. Jay and I had gone to replace her shattered glass, and it took us about the whole time to wheedle the true story out of her. Still, Jay decided not to wait around. He left Tranquility Lane before Vonda could reappear.

Things began going wrong by the next day, and it didn't take long for Jay to decide Vonda had aligned the stars against him. There had been a number of small accidents like his toaster catching fire. His TV acted possessed before it completely shorted out. There was an infestation of Asian ladybugs in his house.

Daddy didn't take serious notice of anything being wrong until Jay suffered a true brush with death. That was when Ivan, our big yellow bull, found a weak spot in the fence and broke into Dwight Russell's field after a cow in heat. I would have waited him out and let him come back when he was ready, but Jay decided to take the trailer over there to load him up and bring him home. As soon as he got the trailer hitched up, he realized it had a flat. He jacked the trailer up, ready to take the tire off, when the brakes on his truck failed and rolled straight into the barn, dragging the trailer off the jack, and almost hauling Jay with it. It took him the rest of the day to fix his brakes and the flat.

He was already worn out when he finally went to pick up Ivan. Jay pulled up close to Ivan in the middle of Dwight's field and spoke his cow talk to that old Limousine bull. Ivan didn't care to argue about it being time to go home. Not after he smelled that sweet apple in Jay's hand. The bull climbed in the trailer and ate his apple, and Jay shut the door and drove home. It seemed like the first good thing to happen to Jay all week, but that changed when Ivan recognized his surroundings. He must have been excited to climb out into his own field, and in the anticipation, he started to jump, the trailer rocking with him. His hind legs kicked up in the air, and his whole body bucked. Just as Jay unlocked the door to let him out, Ivan's hooves struck the metal wall of the trailer. The sharp, banging noise scared him so bad, that when the door opened, the two-ton bull lost his footing, and he slid the rest of the way out. This caused the trailer door to fly backwards, and Jay, who couldn't let go fast enough, got knocked down pretty good. He laid there in a wet cow pile, trying to catch his breath while Ivan found his land legs and high-tailed it back to the herd.

"You could have gotten yourself killed," Daddy said. "You can't trust no bull. I swear. I can't turn my back on either of you boys for a minute." That was typical bluster for Daddy, but for once Jay had nothing to say back.

On Wednesday morning, Jay was awakened by the sharp yips of a red fox. The sound was so close, and so unusual, Jay ran outside in his underwear to see what was happening. Sure enough, there was a red fox chasing his cat Bobby Blue out of the woods and through the orchard.

Bobby Blue was a foundling that had appeared outside of Jay's door soon after Jay moved into granny's old house. He turned out to be the best cat there ever was. Bobby was a good mouser and good company, but most importantly, he was a work cat. No matter what the job, Bobby would always follow along with the aim to help. Sometimes, of course he was just in the way, but he thought he was helping. Daddy said he was the smartest cat he had ever seen. What amazed me was how he liked to find a high spot in the evenings and watch the cattle around Jay's house as if they were his and it was his sole duty to protect the herd. He was afraid of nothing, never knowing when something had the better of him, which was almost the case with the fox.

Jay's bare feet ran into the dewy grass without thinking. Unarmed, he yelled at the fox, which paused, looked confused and continued her short, fast barks. Bobby Blue saw his opportunity to escape and ran straight toward Jay and the safety of the back porch. The fox waited, not sure if it was wise to follow or not. Jay went back in the house and grabbed his grandfather's .22-caliber single shot and a handful of shells. His intent was to shoot just near enough the fox to scare her away. When he stepped outside again, he found the little red beast standing in the same spot. He slid one small shell into the gun barrel and pulled the bolt, locking it in place. But at that moment, with his feet cold and wet from the grass, Jay forgot how to shoot.

The gun raised fast and steady to where his eye and the sight could meet. He aimed at the ground near the little fox's feet, sure to scare it but not wound it. His finger wrapped itself firmly around the trigger and tightened, but the gun remained silent. He lowered the gun from his face and searched its simple mechanisms, but, somehow, his mind was blank as to why it would not shoot. He tried again, repeating each previous action, but the rifle and its one single shot were resolute.

He released the bolt and the unfired shell jumped backwards. He pushed it into place and locked the bolt a second time. But again the gun refused to fire. Jay forgot both times to cock the hammer, and even though he looked directly at it, his mind was so befuddled, that important middle step never occurred to him. He could not think to pull the firing pin.

The fox considered all of this with some patience and only an occasional sharp bark. Jay considered it as well. The sun was brighter after this time, and a slight mist was rising from the ground around him and the fox. Jay was suddenly conscious his feet were naked in the dewy grass. He had given up on shooting at the fox. He decided to wave his arms instead, yelling, "Get. Get out of here. Go on." Finally, the fox turned and skittered back to the woods. When Jay went again towards the house, he found Bobby Blue waiting on the porch steps, impatient for his breakfast, as if none of this was any concern to him.

The next morning, Jay woke to the sound of the fox's noise again. Stepping onto the porch, he called Bobby Blue, but the cat never appeared, and the fox's barks moved further and deeper into the woods. All day, Bobby's breakfast remained uneaten in his bowl, and by night time, Jay had convinced himself the little red devil must have killed and eaten his cat. The absence of the gray farm cat grew burdensome on Jay, and he could not help blame Vonda.

After all this continuous trouble, it was hard for me to argue Vonda hadn't set some demon on his back. Even waking up this morning to only a trickle of water pressure seemed like her doing although a busted water line is the kind of event that could happen to anybody.

Daddy and I went to help Jay with his water trouble. The three of us walked back and forth over the line. We tried to find any kind of damp patch of ground, arguing we were too far over one way or another. Once Daddy spotted it, it seemed like the most obvious thing in the world. The ground was soft from the slow release of so much water, and as Jay's mattock went deeper, the dirt turned right muddy before it became a pure puddle.

For a while, there was only the dull, repeated sound of the mattock striking the earth, and then the steady dragging away of the loose dirt. Jay swung down in short, quick thumps, but not hard enough to cut the water line if he were to hit it by accident.

"Jack, go turn the valve off," Daddy said. The mattock splashed into the mud before Jay's arm would stop. "Looks like we've found it for sure."

I ran down Jay's driveway and across the gravel lane. The gate into the cattle field and the well house door both stood open and waiting. The blue valve turned easy, and I could feel the pressure build in the line, pulsing in my hand like a heart beat, the water waiting to be released again.

By the time I had walked back up to the hole, Jay had dragged most of the mud away from the line. He stood tense then pulled his shoulders down. His back stretched out to relieve the stress. His hair was wooly from what I had figured was another night of restless sleep.

Daddy was already down on his stomach. His hands felt for the puncture in the three-quarter inch plastic as if he were reading Braille.

"Lord God," Daddy said when we heard the sound of a car on the gravel road. Vonda's red Sunfire inched toward the place where we were fixing the water line. Behind her was her man Ligon Fields in his rusted-out Ford pickup. Ligon styled himself a preacher, although he was always the first to tell you he had no official training besides what the Lord had given him. He had a regular following, even though he had to sit out from preaching every now and then. For sooner or later, he got caught stealing money or sleeping with a deacon's wife. And once or twice, he'd been arrested for fighting chickens. But Ligon was the kind of man that took such things in stride, laying low for a while and then finding an empty church building, calling in the faithful from his past congregations and starting up again.

Vonda's head turned back and forth from the road in front of her while trying to see us up in the driveway. The car stopped, and she motioned me towards her. I just waved and turned my attention completely to the muddy hole in front of me, pretending I didn't realize she wanted me to come down to her.

"If we ignore them, maybe they'll go away," I said.

Without waiting any time, the Sunfire sputtered up the little incline of Jay's driveway and into the grass as close as she could get to where we worked. Ligon pulled his truck up behind her until their bumpers almost kissed.

"You made me drive all the way up here on this hill, and now I'll have to throw this parking brake."

"Vonda, now's not the best time," Daddy said.

"The Lord don't wait for the time of man," Vonda told us. She climbed out of the car's low seat. "Besides, I'm not looking for you. I'm here to see Jay. I hear he's had enough trouble for a while and we've come to save him from eternal misery."

"Howdy Ligon," Daddy said from the ground as Ligon stepped closer. "You out saving souls today?" Daddy's hands were still down in the mud, trying to fit in a new piece of plastic line where he had cut out the old piece with the crack. When he looked up, his eyes stuck on a Ziploc bag Ligon carried full of white powder.

"Well, I save when I can," Ligon said, smiling. He was as slim a man as I had ever seen, his skin tough and leathery.

"I reckon there's still a lot out there that needs it."

"The souls are out there all right. But you've got to be like a tom cat and make the calls."

"Well there ain't no need of making a call here," Jay said. "You two can go on home."

"Lord, now I know you're just trying to vex my spirit," Vonda said. "And here I am come to help you."

"I don't want no more help from you. That's what got me in this mess to begin with." Jay's face started to color.

"Hush up boy. I brought Ligon up here to end your suffering."

"What with? A bag of sugar?"

"This ain't sugar," Ligon answered in a tone suggesting Jay should know better. "This is salt of the earth. Salt from which we all come. And from which we shall all return."

"Sugar or salt, you can put it away. I'm not going in for none of your voodoo."

Vonda grabbed for the bag as Ligon's arms went straight up. For a moment, I thought he was going to hit Jay, but Ligon opened his palm and laid it on Jay's forehead, his long fingers extended around Jay's skull in a death grip. "You listen to me boy. An evil spirit has ridden an ill wind and sat down on your soul, and I'm here to get him out whether you want me to or not. Now close your eyes and pray, dammit."

Vonda's hand reached into the snowy powder and then flew out to scatter the salt in a circle around their feet. She threw and threw while Ligon began praying aloud.

"Devil I rebuke ye in the name of the Lord," he started, but he progressed into such a fast, high-pitched whine, the words all jumbled together so that only God could understand them fully. I thought maybe this was what it meant to speak in tongues. The whole time Vonda's wrinkled little fingers went in and out of the salt, flicking the crystals onto Jay's and Ligon's feet, while her own legs danced in a circle around them.

I couldn't tell what effect this was having on Jay, although it surprised me he remained standing in the middle of this mess, with Ligon's hand pushing firmly down on his head and Vonda pelting him with salt.

Daddy's hands had finally stopped moving in the freshly dug hole. His entire body became still, watching the proceedings.

I was mesmerized, sure the flames would leap up from the ground at any moment. Everything in my head seemed to run together. I felt like I was walking in darkness, feeling my way forward with one foot before the other. I was afraid of falling down. And in my mind's eye, I saw Vonda throwing handfuls of pure fire from her magic bag and onto Jay. I went to step forward, but I felt overpowered by the sudden darkness. It had seemed to overtake everything around me until I wasn't sure which way to go. I moved forward, but I don't remember ever being so afraid to fall. My heart beat to the rhythm of Ligon's voice, which grasped for breath as his face and neck grew redder.

Out of nowhere, that fox began to bark. The noise called me back from my imaginings, and I looked across the road and into the field. Down by the creek, I saw a gray streak followed by a red flash of fire. That crazy little fox was chasing Bobby Blue, barking like a regular dog, but at a higher, eerier octave.

Ligon paused in his prayer. Vonda stopped her dance. Jay took the opportunity to step away from Ligon's reach, and even Daddy stood up to get a better look across the field.

Bobby Blue jumped across the creek and then paused to see if the fox was still following.

"Come on, Bobby," Jay yelled. "Come here."

The fox sat across the water and stared boldly up the path Bobby made through the cattle field, his lithe body swimming gracefully through the spring grass.

Jay moved farther away from us and closer to the cat. "Where have you been?" he asked from the other side of his yard. Jay sat down in the grass to pet Bobby's blue gray back. Neither of the two paid the fox any more attention, and at some moment when I wasn't looking, that fox disappeared.

"Well I guess that's the end of that," Daddy said as he lowered himself back down to the ground.

"And I guess we better hit the road," Ligon said, making long strides back to his truck and looking to the sky. It was hard to tell if he felt insulted or just recognized when his job was finished. "Looks like more rain's coming," he said, mostly to himself as he walked away.

"Might do it," Daddy answered, but not loud enough that Ligon or Vonda either one would hear. Bent down, his hands tightened the hose clamps he had already secured around the line. "It might do it."

"You all go home with us," Vonda said as she walked back to her car. The half-empty bag of salt hung limply by her side. "I've got a good mess of beans cooked." There was nothing but sweetness in her voice. She opened the car door but stopped before getting in.

"We better get this water running again," I said. "But thanks anyway."

Daddy and I watched their vehicles back slowly down the hill and make their way out of the lane, driving by Jay and his cat.

"What in the world?" was all I could say to Daddy.

With his eye moving from Ligon's truck to Vonda's red car, Daddy said, almost to himself, "Those two beat more than you can stick a bucket under. But at least they've got conviction. You've got to give them that." His hands were muddy, and he rubbed them together to remove the moisture.

I was unsure of what we had witnessed that day, even of what I had felt happen to myself. I didn't expect Daddy believed much of Ligon's show, but it was hard to even talk about it.

"If he feels better is all that counts," Daddy finally said.

Jay never said for sure what he thought about that visit from Ligon and Vonda, but that day I watched him lie in the grass, so relaxed he reminded me of what he looked like as a little boy. Bobby Blue climbed over his chest until their heads rubbed against each other. That was the first time in a long while I heard laughter from Jay.

Randall Brown

The Celebrity

H E GLOWS, MY SON SAID OF THE CELEBRITY. We met him on the tennis court, my son a twelve-year-old tennis prodigy, his serve a swerving, unhittable blur of ball and racquet.

My son noticed him on the bench. At the net, he whispered, "He's watching me."

My son made the Celebrity the star-gazer—and my nobodyness grew with each of my son's aces, his top-spin lobs, his passing shots from beyond the baseline.

"Kid," the Celebrity said, when it ended. "You are something."

They set a time to play, the following morning. It rained overnight, but when we arrived the staff had squeegeed the court, and now knelt, wiping the excess with towels.

I heard someone speak once of the defeated heavyweight fighter, about his diminishment, his fall from gianthood. I thought of that as ball after ball sailed into the net, over the line, behind him, finally one glancing off his racquet into his eye, knocking him down. They swarmed over him, brought ice. He shoved them away, made his solitary way back to his cottage, swaying as if drunk.

"Jeez, he sucked," my son said.

We received, that night, an invitation to dinner. A boat took us to a private island used by the hotel. A pig roasted in a pit. The Celebrity, men and women who were his friends or part of the entourage, and us.

"I bet you didn't know we could get black eyes," he said to my son, speaking not of celebrities but of black people.

"I never thought about it," my son answered.

"If you were a stock, I'd invest in you," the Celebrity said. "You've got someday written all over you."

"Thanks," my son said. A waiter brought him another virgin mango and banana daiquiri, brought me another drink I couldn't name.

It ended with white fireworks, like an explosion of stars. We sat on the edge of the ocean. My son put his arm around me.

"What do you think, Dad? About what he said. That someday stuff."

I watched the sky. The Caribbean waves like ripples from a stone thrown far off. They sounded like the tiny splashes of my son in the bathtub. One night, I had sat with him, the water draining out, thinking of death of all things. With his finger he'd touched my tears, tasted them, asked what it was.

"Salt," I had said.

Always, after that, he'd asked for tears to put on his eggs, his fries... what was I trying to remember? —to say? Don't grow up. Forget about someday.

"Dad? Do you think he's right?"

"Of course," I said. "Anyone can see that."

"That's cool," he said, then pointed down the beach.

The Celebrity stood alone, at the ocean's edge. I wondered about his loneliness, his secret wishes, his life here among the mortals. He knelt. It looked as if he were building something, dribbling wet sand, over and over again.

B. J. Best

egg toss

we stand at the cusp of a line
in the yard of a fourth of july,
cradling our babies closer

than an oyster polishing its pearl.
but soon, upon orders, they must sail:
these uncooked chicks, these uncashed

checks, these unhatched desires like a squadron
of stars constellating the evening with the terror
of flight. we hope our partner

who is paces away knows her patience;
the scoop, catch, and glide; the body
and the things that beat there.

thus, through the night
spangled with humidity, flows
the arc of a conversation

that sounds something like prayer:
don't let me fall; don't let me
shatter; pool me in your soft hands

so i may never fly from you again.

fingernails

my wife tends the small garden of her hands:
weeding the edges, soothing the soil.
soon, the flowers of her fingers bloom poppy-red,
then the petals fall off in soft flakes.

the fields of my hands have been kept
by a farmer with an affinity for bourbon.
where the lifeline is furrowed, you can see
where his tractor veered three separate times.

he has not yet cut firewood from the broken trees
of my freckles rotting behind the white hills
of my knuckles. the patchy flax on my fingers
has yet to be harvested, and the joints creak

like rusting springs of his truck.
these january nights, our house is bitter as hay.
my wife keeps the bulbs of her thumbs shooting
in the greenhouse of our electric blanket.

lit by a gray moon, i study my hand, the hangnails
standing like snowmen. my fingernails
are five frozen ponds at the edge of that field.
you can imagine a couple ice-skating there,

carving their curlicues, discussing what
they should grow in the summer: beans, maybe;
red peppers the rabbits will eat; or a child
whose hands they will forever tend together.

B. J. Best

sudden prayer for my mailbox

curled in the corner of the cul-de-sac
and the scent of sweet august grass,
it stands like the head of a hammer,

ready to bang its telegraphs to the world.
sometimes it raises its red hand,
so excited for the postmaster to call on it;

other times i open its mouth and it yawns
like a lion, bored with three days of no news.
it's a brown trout pregnant with thin fingerlings,

a safe where the stamps glitter like jewels.
in this life, i would like to take whatever
is sent to me, read it in the language

in which it is written, work for days
on the words of my reply. but often
my heart is a wolf with no forwarding address,

tromping through snow, hunting too hard.
o holy barn of my business, o black hole
at the center of the mailman's faith:

let me learn to love my last name;
the zip code of my coats' zippers; and
the omelets i'm making for breakfast:

red peppers in their envelopes of egg
to be mailed in care of my wife
at the dining room table, her bathrobe

wrapped around her like a package
i'm excited to open right there
in the bright post office of morning.

shooting star

it is a golf shot of god,
a quick line of cocaine,
the eyelash of an angel
burning into a tear.
and so the orphans are amazed,
the cows look up from their cud.
you'd like to catch
that blistering egg
in the empty baskets of your eyes,
but you blink and you miss,
its yolk broken like moonlight
all over your jeans.

B. J. Best

pollen

all summer long, the wind
is spreading the seeds
of your sneezes, and your eyes
keep on weeping as if
they've seen a god.
no, scratch that—you pop
your antihistamines as if they were
the body of jesus, and you
like a zealot needing
to sniff more of this snuff,
convinced that your wheezing
is leading you somewhere,
such as the garden of sunflowers
that could be—
but aren't quite—elysian.

Susan Lilley

Swing

Somewhere along the line I stopped swinging
and have almost forgotten how it feels
to sweep the ground with my own hair
leaning back on the plain plank seat
under the waning sun, arms straight,
hands on the creaking ropes, pushing
gravity away with my feet
in an upside-down flight to the top
of some invisible pinnacle, a long second
of impossible geometric standstill, toes touching
the gold leaves of the oak's most down-
gestured branch. The callow twilight
pinks up the sky and I am so nearsighted
that the world is dreamspotted
like a Monet. It will be another year
before glasses are prescribed and I see
individual leaves on trees and
the certainty of death.
But at ten, my eyes slitted against the rich
wind, I listen to the ropes and distant,
air-borne voices, my parents young
and always alive across the blurred hedge,
talking of dinner and trimming azaleas.

Caitlin Militello

The Flower of Summer

EVERY DAY ON THE WAY BACK from his middle school Takuo passed the strange old house that was a cross between the aristocratic style and an abomination. There was something about the place and its ornamentation and scale that was, inexplicably, a little too big, or a little too much, or a little bit the wrong angle: variations so slight nothing should have been wrong with it, and yet it somehow was an architectural horror.

"That old eyesore," his mother would lament when Takuo reported to her any minor changes. The fence, lately, had fallen into disrepair. "Any house of that style ought to have a stone wall around it, not a wooden fence!" she would say. "All those beautiful buildings and temples we lost in the war and earthquakes and fires, and yet such hideous places never lose so much as a shingle. True beauty, Takuo, is never long for this earth!" Then, as if willing herself to be among those truly beautiful things, she would complain of some malady or other and go to the couch for a rest.

The house of Ooshio Takuo, she never failed to remind him, was the model of taste, rebuilt by his father before Takuo had been born so that it was exactly as their family home had been for generations, but for the convenient modern adaptations he'd allowed for in the design.

The other house was owned by a man named Shibata, who made a fortune selling overpriced sake to good teahouses like the one belonging to Takuo's family. Though it was necessary their families be on good terms, Takuo's mother knew restraint only when it was required of her; when there was no one but the two of them at home she was happy to criticize Shibata's poor taste and what she referred to as slick character.

"What can he be doing all day," she would ask, Takuo knowing he was never to try and answer, "making the sake with his own hands? Harvesting the rice from the fields? People say his wife is alone almost all the time, and that he forbids her to go out!"

She had even brought it up recently to Takuo's father, to which he had replied very simply, "Well, she is quite a beauty." Takuo's mother seemed, after that, to be disinclined to mention it to him again.

Since that evening, however, Takuo had been increasingly curious about the wife of this tasteless Mr. Shibata. He had, throughout his years of middle school, seen glimpses of her within the house, or heard her rattling around in the yard behind the fence. It seemed from Takuo's patchwork experience with this woman he did not know that she rather enjoyed the garden, as he had once glimpsed her back and thin but roundish posterior laboring in the ground, a plain white robe tucked tight around her hips. He was not familiar then with what was pleasing in the shapes of women, but he wondered if what he saw had something to do with his father's comment, or if she had a small and stunning face like the geisha at his father's tea house.

He preferred to think of her this way, this woman whose face he had never seen: that she was a beauty with a countenance like a poem has eloquence. He wondered whether it was not the home of a woman of mere beauty but of purity, of perfection, as he passed the ugly house each morning and afternoon.

It was not long before Takuo, in his clean and proper middle school uniform, developed the dirty and improper habit of peeping. He was, naturally, not the only person to travel those streets, and therefore had to be careful. He developed certain habits that might make his loitering there seem permissible—his bag needed adjusting, his books were heavy, the trees hanging over the fence made for the perfect place to relax in the shade or have a small snack. Once or twice some older ladies had caught him with his face nearly painted onto the fence, but it was the one time in his life when his size, below average for his age, was a blessing to him.

"Excuse me, what are you doing?" one lady had asked, clearly appalled. He thought, all at once, of the good relations necessary between his family and the family of Mr. Shibata, of his mother's opinion of the man, of the shame creeping up to his ears and his father's soft face as he answered, without looking, that Mr. Shibata's wife was quite a beauty.

He was too young and innocent, despite all his furtive plans to spy on the beautiful woman, to come up with a decent excuse, and so he told the ladies in the voice of a child, mouth unnaturally rounded with the horror he felt then, that he had heard there was a beautiful woman living at that house, and he'd only wanted to see if it was true.

The blood pounded so hard in his ears he could hardly hear as they laughed, or see that they looked to one another with smiles. They'd taken him for a first year boy with a simple, child's crush.

"How sweet," said one. The tone of their voices had changed completely.

"Have you seen her yet?" asked the other.

He shook his head no, and looked down in shame.

It was deep into summer before Takuo ever saw the face of Mr. Shibata's wife. He interpreted it as great fortune on his part when the woman took to sitting in the shade of her garden each afternoon, so that she was there almost every day when Takuo passed by on his way home, or would emerge from the darkened aberration that was the Shibata house shortly after his arrival at her fence. By that time he'd found all the good splinters and gaps and would sit in the shadow of an overhanging tree, reading a book as though enjoying the pleasant weather, pretending to loosen the collar of his uniform as he turned his head to the side to gaze at her. As far as he knew she was never aware of his presence, for such a proper and elegant lady would never participate in something so scandalous with intention, surely. Takuo was very young yet, and not aware that all beautiful women, though properly delicate on the outside, were not all gentle, fragile flowers on the inside, or that there are all kinds of good reasons for doing something that make it improper only on the outside.

His father's assessment of Mr. Shibata's wife had not been false. When Takuo saw her face at last he felt as though he'd been given new eyes, ones that contained all the visions and experiences of his old ones but that were capable of seeing so much more. Where his old eyes had once seen beautiful women with thin, soft skin and narrow-smiling lips, his new eyes saw all these things in a grander scheme, an earth-sized net of breathtaking things all connected and building on one another, where some of the eyelets were crammed full of things and most of the others stared back at him emptily, waiting to be filled. Mr. Shibata's wife, unlike all the beautiful women he had been near before who were crammed in up to the twine of a few common looking eyelets, was on a tier of her own, filling every space and gap and coloring the things around her a soft, delicate shade of a color he had no name for. His new eyes saw, too, that the emotionless look of his father, that night he had answered his mother regarding the hermitage of Mr. Shibata's wife, was not a look of indifference but the face of restraint.

Mr. Shibata's wife, Takuo thought, is the most beautiful woman in the world. If those older ladies could have seen him now, his cheeks flush, the sweat percolating on his brow, his collar growing damp. His heaving chest felt disconnected from his body.

Mr. Shibata's wife, he thought again, is the most beautiful woman in the world. And thanks to Mr. Shibata's wife, his concept of the world was expanding like the ocean eating up the shore. It seemed, suddenly, an endless place, beyond the tea houses and his school and the streets he knew.

He did not know her name and there was no one he could ask without raising suspicion, so he began to call her Ajisai, meaning hydrangea flower, after the startling blue and purple blooms that grew in his yard each year. The ajisai, his mother said, never bloomed long enough to satisfy, so that she had to look forward to the pleasure of seeing them each year.

The truly beautiful is fleeting, he had come to believe, like the ajisai in summer, and each day he looked forward to the time when he would see her again, the most beautiful woman in the world whom he called the name of a flower.

Takuo hadn't, at first, noticed Ajisai's rounded belly. As the weeks went on and her face, too, began to appear less narrow, he saw the correlation and realized the young woman was to become a mother. He wasn't sure how this fit into his image of her as the perfect woman, so he ignored her distortions and continued to sit by her fence, gazing in at her when no one was looking and it seemed an opportune moment to adjust his collar.

In time he began to notice a sadness about her, a lonely feeling cast off from her downward-angled eyes as definitely as if it were tears. The net of his world, big and consuming as it was, was after all full of holes and unable to contain things by its nature. Her sadness was the first thing he realized it could not hope to contain.

He tried to find reasons why she was lonely, some of them childish and some of them more astute: she was too eager to see the face of the baby inside her, and it made her feel lonely that she had to carry what must have been such a beautiful child all the time without ever seeing it; she was lonely for Mr. Shibata, who left her alone all day even though she was carrying his first child for him; she missed her relatives whom she could not go off to see as she was forbidden to go around; she was lonely because she was idle, unable to tend to her beautiful garden as she so loved now that the baby was growing within her; she had been waiting all her life for someone with eyes as keen as Takuo to see her and understand her beauty as no one else could.

In his stupider moments he chucked flowers from his mother's garden over the fence when she was not there, so that she might find them and be pleased. He thought about writing her a letter once or twice, but knew it would be out of the question and that she'd be on the lookout for her admirer if he went through with it, and then it would all be spoiled. In the end he could only conclude, and perhaps there was even a little truth to it, that very beautiful women, on account of being in a class of their own, were doomed to a certain unebbing solitude. There would always be someone like Mr. Shibata in their lives, who distrusted them because they were so very beautiful, though they simply could not help it.

But this, he would learn in future years, was not the case for his Ajisai. As an adult he would look back on her thick, downcast eyelashes and bent neck as she sat sweating delicately in the shade of her garden, and recognize her expression as the succumbing mixture of loneliness and guilt. That summer, however, she was to be a holy vision in Takuo's eyes, a goddess of pure and divine beauty, until the faint wind of August, hot and fat with moisture, would sweep in and alter his perceptions forever. When Takuo's school began its summer recess he was distraught over how to casually continue his visits to Ajisai's fence. After a lot of careful consideration he came to believe that, if the shade of the trees from her yard really made for the prime reading spot he had pretended it to be all this time, there was no reason a bookish young boy should give it up just because school was out of session. To be safe, however, he tried not to go every day, and took a different book along though he hadn't read a page of the first one.

Her belly had gotten so big by then that it was impossible to ignore, and he had begun to incorporate it into his dreams and wakeful, though mostly innocent fantasies. In one daydream he had met her on the street as she walked, parasol in hand, with Mr. Shibata, and Takuo with his mother. They exchanged greetings and small talk, his mother inquiring about the baby. Then Ajisai, mistaking him as the older ladies had done for a younger boy, would ask if he'd like to touch her belly, or put his ear to it, the question alternating depending on the day he dreamt it. He would always reach forward, shyly, and put his hand softly against her silk kimono, which was always splendid and never made her sweat a drop, and through it he would imagine he could feel the softness of her skin. The belly was surprisingly firm, and when he touched it he would know there was a beautiful baby inside.

Once or twice her breath had figured into his fantasy, tickling the back of his neck or ears as he gingerly touched Ajisai's stomach. He found this addition a little uncomfortable, however, and so most of the time imagined the coolness of the shade from her parasol, and the excitement of being so close to someone so perfect. Takuo knew that this sort of privilege would be granted only to a very small child, and it was then that he would realize, with a disturbing start, that in his fantasies he *was* a small child, the hand that reached for Ajisai brown with sun and the fingers short and stubby, and he would wake from his dreams in dismay. He tried, more than once, to picture himself as a grown man, old enough to have married Ajisai instead of Mr. Shibata, but he could not imagine what kind of man he would be or how he would look at that age, and quickly gave up on the attempt.

One afternoon, that August, he arrived before Ajisai did. He heard the familiar grinding of wood against wood as she slid the side doors of the house open, the clatter as she slipped her tiny but swollen feet into her geta and clunked carefully across the stones, each day a little slower than before as her belly grew more cumbersome. Someone, perhaps Mr. Shibata, had set out a chair for her, the back against a tree, so that she could sit comfortably and enjoy the garden without the strain of rising from the ground each time she wished to leave. Takuo, again almost in disbelief of his good luck, had a perfect view of his Ajisai where she now sat in front of the tree.

He could see with his sharp eyes the folds of the fabric of her yukata, a light pink with a tasteful pattern of sparrows, and could see the places where it stuck to her pale chest from sweat. She fanned herself like the perfect lady and admired the garden around her. Then she sat forward, moving her knees apart so the bulk of her belly could fall between her thighs, and untied the sash on her garment.

Takuo watched it all with wide eyes, his book and all his pretenses forgotten on the grass beside him. The net of his world, he thought, was about to burst. He was going to see her pregnant belly, he thought with bizarre excitement, and pressed his face up against the fence, trying hard not to breathe lest she hear something and catch him. He was in rapture as she uncoiled the obi from around her, her yukata falling slowly open around her chest. At last she pulled the sash away from her body, folded it neatly, and draped it over an arm of the chair.

The perfect woman… he thought in synch with the pounding of his heart. The most beautiful woman in the world, the most beautiful… Her skin was so very pale where he could see it. He tried to wait patiently, even casually, picking up his book again and throwing it open in a distracted way, waiting with a furiously drumming heart for the yukata to fall open as she sunk back into the chair, fanning herself as though she couldn't tolerate the heat a second longer. Takuo couldn't believe his great luck might run out at this of all moments, so he tried to calm himself a little and put his back to the fence.

More than once it occurred to him that he may be doing something wrong, but that thought was tied to a belief that propriety, in the shade of Ajisai's garden, was no longer relevant.

At last, to his good fortune and ardent distress, the woman threw open her cotton robe, heaving a sigh that made her whole body seize like a savage and indelicate animal. She was naked beneath the yukata.

Takuo felt his stomach lurch.

That beautiful belly, the one which surely contained a baby of the most exquisite sort, was huge and veiny. The place where her belly button should have been was stretched and disfigured, marred by red marks as though angry. Her breasts, breasts that should have been perfect, were instead huge and grotesque, the nipples purple, gigantic, her inflated body a nightmare he hadn't begun to have and could not wake from. He stared, horrified, at the dark space between her legs, and began to shake. She was spoiled for him.

Mr. Shibata had spoiled the perfect flower of summer that should have belonged to Takuo's sharp, admiring eyes alone. Takuo thought, in that moment, that he had learned true hatred, perfect hatred in accord with the ruin of the perfect beauty, but he was not yet aware that jealousy could exist where the object of desire was not really his at all, and not for something like a fountain pen or some other equally unimportant object.

Jealousy, his mother had once told him, was an ugly and tasteless trait. As one with such wonderful taste and an eye for beauty he did not know he was capable of such utter ugliness, compared to which Mr. Shibata's tacky house was nothing.

Always act nobly, she said, with pride and honor. He thought himself honorable for hating Mr. Shibata, who so deserved it for the wreckage he'd made of Ajisai's perfection.

True beauty, he thought, is fleeting.

He tried to forget Ajisai, telling himself that he was only interested in what was then beautiful. He soon started high school and no longer would pass her fence, nor wish to gaze at the white nape of her long neck. Her beauty was like the sparrows on her pink yukata that day, noticeable but quick to fly away, delicate, indeed, but not as delicate as other birds. He wanted to find a woman with beauty like the crane, who, it was said in legends, was able to live a thousand years.

No matter how often he told himself these things, at night he still saw her: her swollen belly, her dark, enlarged nipples. In his dreams he would reach for them, not knowing which he wanted to touch first, and falter. She would smile gently at him, encouraging him, ignorant at how ugly and gross he thought her body. But he, too, was ignorant. He did not know why but no matter how repulsive she seemed he still reached for her every time, a strange, gruesome temptation he could not resist. In some of his dreams he was a little boy, reaching to feel her belly, trying to suckle from her oversized nipples while she laughed like a songbird and told him he was too old. Then, suddenly, he would become a full grown man and she was frightened as he put his hands on her and groped desperately for her glossy black hair, sinking his hands in behind her hair pin with a groan.

Ajisai, he whispered with a full-throated greed, calling her by the name he had given her. Her lips quivered and she tried to pull away from him but her back was to the tree.

When her swollen belly brushed against his flat stomach, it was then he realized he was no longer that gentle little boy but a big, brutish man, with a face so lovely and smooth he should have been as handsome as she, and yet there was something profoundly ugly about him. Afraid, he pulled his hands away and stepped back, running his fingers over his own perfect but not beautiful face.

Try as he might, when he awoke from the dream in a sweat he could not tell what was wrong with that face that had become his. He could not, even, remember the way it had looked.

True beauty is fleeting, he thought.

But, he said to himself, in a moment of dazed clarity, true beauty should also be haunting, and cursed himself for the blindness of his new eyes.

The Twin Cities
A Century Ago

An essay in photos

Daily Globe.

VOL. XVIII.—PRICE TWO CENTS—|.......| ST. PAUL, MINN., TUESDAY MORNING, MARCH 26, 1895.   PRICE TWO CENTS—|.......|—NO. 85.

Pictured opposite is the lake in Loring Park. Today it is the largest park in the heart of Minneapolis, bordered by the Basilica of St. Mary, the Walker Arts Center and sculpture garden, and Minneapolis Community and Technical College.

Purchased by the city in the late 1800s, the land was previously farmed by Joseph and Nellie Johnson. It was at one time refered to as the Central Park of Minneapolis.

St. Paul and Minneapolis are known as the Twin Cities, and—as with most siblings—a contentious rivalry occasionally rears its ugly head. In 1895, there was an attempt to wrestle the state capitol away from St. Paul and relocate it to Loring Park.

Ultimately, the move was never put to a popular vote in part because of a host of legal obstacles. Although the city had purchased the land for a couple hundred thousand dollars, it had already borrowed millions in mortgages against the land. Many of the deeds and mortgages stated the land must be used as a park. Judge Flandrau stated it would be an indignity to the state to put the capitol on land so indebted.

It was also argued that when Minnesota was split off from Iowa and Wisconsin, St. Paul was specifically named the capitol. When Henry Hastings Sibley was named the first governor of Minnesota, Judge Douglass, one of the men presiding over the territories, offered to let Sibley build the capitol next to his home near Fort Snelling in Mendota, Minnesota. Governor Sibley declined, saying he would abide the initial appointment of St. Paul.

GREEDY MINNIE.

She Makes Her Arguments for Removal of the State Capitol.

JUDGE FLANDRAU DEFENDS

St. Paul—Cites the Compact Made in the Early Days of Minnesota.

A FAIR DIVISION OF SPOILS

The Capitol, University and Penitentiary Were Placed by Pioneers.

EXECUTIVE SESSION HELD

By the Committee and Their Decision Reserved Until Thursday.

The judiciary committee of the house heard talk last night upon the proposition of Minneapolis to offer Loring park for a capitol site. The meeting was held in the house of representatives. There were a number of gentlemen from the two cities present, most of whom wore solemn or indifferent faces, but a few of them were animated in appearance, particularly Judge Flandrau, the veteran jurist and old pioneer of the state, who was present to make a speech against the ability of a city to donate a park, and Solomon Cohen, with ruddy face, who was expected to make the big argument—to annihilate Judge Flandrau. He was very much animated when he rose to speak. The room was half-filled with representatives of both cities. Among those from the city of propositions were Mayor Pratt, C. J. Rockwood, Judge Fish, T. H. Shevelin and representatives of the legislature. Among the St. Paul citizens were members of the house, the venerable ex-Gov. Ramsey, J. A. Wheelock, George Thompson, George C. Squires, A. H. Lindeke, D. R. Noyes, C. N. Bell and D. R. McGinnis, of the Commercial club.

The Minnesota State Fair has long been a great tradition as the biggest gathering in the midwest. In 2009, the fair drew 1.8 million attendees. F. Scott Fitzgerald, who was born and raised in St. Paul, Minnesota at the turn of the last century, re-created the Minnesota State Fair in a story set in 1909. (The grandstand photo below is dated 1906, the state fair "traffic jam" on the page opposite is from 1912, while the midway photo split on the following pages was taken in 1917.)

"*The two cities were separated only by a thin well-bridged river; their tails curling over the banks met and mingled, and at the juncture, under the jealous eye of each, lay, every fall, the State Fair. Because of its advantageous position, and because of the agricultural eminence of the state, the fair was one of the most magnificent in America. There were immense exhibits of grain, livestock and farming machinery; there were horse races and automobile races and, lately, aeroplanes that really left the ground; there was a tumultuous Midway with Coney Island thrillers to whirl you through space, and a whining, tinkling hoochie-coochie show. As a compromise between the serious and the trivial, a grand display of fireworks, culminating in a representation of the Battle of Gettysburg, took place in the Grand Concourse every night.*"
   —"A Night at the Fair" F. Scott Fitzgerald,
     July 21, 1928 Saturday Evening Post.

Holtzermann's Chicago Store sold dry goods and specialized in German toys (Deutsche Spielwaaren) prior to World War I. The store was established by Louis J. and J.D. Holtzermann in 1887. The store resided near the current locations of the University of Minnesota Twin Cities Carlson School of Management and Augsburg College.

Many children of this generation had fond memories of making the trip downtown during the holidays to buy gilded Christmas decorations, mechanized toy animals made of tin, music boxes and cuckoo clocks, tin soldiers, and dolls with eyelids that opened and closed.

On the page opposite, a horse-drawn fire engine races past the store on the way to a fire in 1907.

The Palace Museum (pictured opposite at Marquette and Washington Avenues in Minneapolis, 1896) was one of a series of dime museums that opened up in the 1880s and 1890s. The first dime museum was opened by P. T. Barnum. Dime museums hosted traveling acts, illusionists, palmists, psychics, and mysterious "oddities" as well as the occasional concert or play.

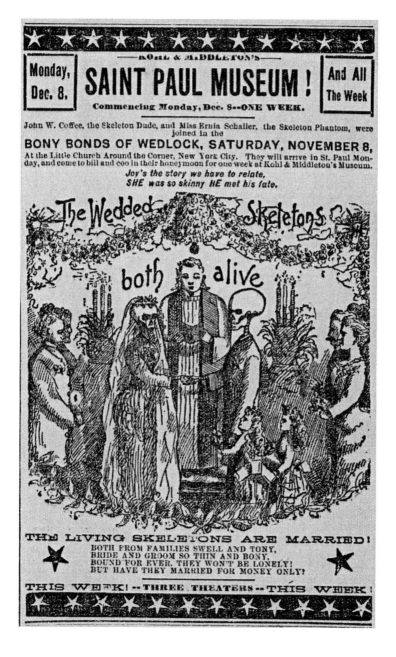

Nicollet Ave and 5th, looking toward the river, 1898.

Traffic jam on Nicollet Ave and 6th Street, 1905.

Lake Harriet in Minneapolis was named after Harriet Lovejoy, the wife of Col. Henry Leavenworth who lived in Fort Snelling. Colonel Leavenworth fougth in the War of 1812 and established Fort Leavenworth in Kansas. The lake and surrounding land was donated to the city by William S. King, a U.S. Representative and journalist who helped found the *Star Tribune* and *St. Pioneer Press* newspapers.

The first Lake Harriet Pavilion was opened in 1888 (see ad from *St. Paul Daily Globe*). That pavilion burned down in 1891. The new pavilion, pictured above was then constructed and was successful until it, too, burned down in 1903, a year after this photo was taken. Another pavilion was built in 1904 and lasted twenty years before it was destroyed in a windstorm. A bandshell still exists at this site after a number of re-builds, and was most recently rennovated by a neighborhood group in 2004.

LAKE HARRIET PAVILION.

LAKE HARRIET PAVILION

GRAND OPENING
By Danz's Military Band

Saturday Evening, June 30th, from 8 to 10 O'clock.

Motor Trains from Washington Avenue every TEN MINUTES, from 7 to 8 o'clock p. m., Fare ten cents, each way. *Seats in the Auditorium Free!* Sunday afternoon and evening, July 1st, a special Sacred Concert will be given by Danz's Military Band, beginning at 2 and 8 o'clock p. m. SEATS FREE.

FOURTH OF JULY!

A Special Patriotic Programme will be rendered by the Danz Military Band, beginning at 2 and 8 o'clock p. m., also a Gorgeous Display of Fireworks, unequaled in grandeur and brilliancy. Trains every ten minutes; fare, ten cents each way. Seats in Auditorium FREE!

A Free Concert will be given in the Pavilion every evening and Sunday afternoon during the season by Danz's Military Band; also, Special Attractions will be furnished from time to time. The beautiful grove connected with the Pavilion can be secured at any time, free of charge, for picnic purposes on application to the undersigned.

A. O. HOYT, Manager.

Pictured opposite is the opening of Selby Tunnel on August 10, 1907. The new tunnel allowed streetcars to climb the steep grade from the lower business district of St. Paul along the river up to the Summit Ave residence area. Prior to this tunnel, the streetcars were only able to negotiate the hill with a series of cables, pulleys, and counterweights that made the short journey a time-consuming one.

Today Summit Ave. boasts the longest remaining stretch (five miles) of residential Victorian architecture in the United States. It overlooks the Mississippi River, the state capitol building, and is home to the Cathedral of St. Paul. The empire builder James J. Hill of the Great Northern Railroad lived here and his home remains open as a museum. F. Scott Fitzgerald also lived on Summit Hill.

"There is a sloping midsection of our city which lies between the residence quarter on the hill and the business district on the level of the river. It is a vague part of town, broken by its climb into triangles and odd shapes—there are names like Seven Corners—and I don't believe a dozen people could draw an accurate map of it, though everyone traversed it by trolley, auto or shoe leather twice a day."
—F. Scott Fitzgerald, "A Short Trip Home"
December 17, 1927 *Saturday Evening Post*

Pictured below is Lake Street Bridge in 1907. It spans the Mississippi from Minneapolis to St. Paul. When the wrought-iron span bridge was built in 1889, the *Minneapolis Tribune* called it a "foolish extravagence" as there were already bridges crossing nearby. Eventually the Lake Street bridge became the oldest bridge still in use over the Mississippi. At one time it carried a major artery (U.S. Route 212) between the cities, and it wasn't re-built until a hundred years later. When workers tried to demolish the old bridge, initial attempts failed to take the bridge down and it took several attempts over the next couple weeks with increased levels of explosives. When the I-35 bridge collapsed in 2007, the bridge helped relieve traffic flow in the highway's absence.

Alison Baker

I'll Meet You There

H E DRIVES, SHE NAVIGATES. Everything is dry and bright. There are many, many cars, there is a long highway, there are billboards and there are low flat houses clustered together with nothing between them and the sun but flat red roofs. Each house sits in a gravel yard, adorned here and there with an artistic grouping of large rocks and a few cacti.

"I can't wait any longer." Williams turns off the highway onto a gravel road that runs past one of these little housing developments and pulls over beside a scramble of bushes and broken glass. When he opens the car door and springs out, the heat pours in around him. Marian listens to his pee sizzle as it hits the ground.

"Marian, could you get me my camera?" Within seconds of stepping into the desert, Williams has found a rattlesnake. "I knew I shouldn't have put it in the trunk."

She gets out of the car, looking carefully at the ground before she puts her feet down, and walks around to the trunk, sure that at any moment something will squirm under her feet, and she opens the trunk and shoves the suitcase around so she can reach the zipper. She pulls out the camera case and takes the camera out of it and then walks on as little of the surface of her feet as she can over to where Williams is grinning at the snake.

"Here," she says.

She doesn't hurry back to the car, though. She stands in the heat and looks out at the landscape, which is ugly. The yards are coated with blinding green grass and the unimproved ground surrounding the development is brown, dusty dirt. Above them the sky is an unlikely blue and there are no clouds. She is ready to turn around and drive back to the airport and take the next plane to a cooler, duller state when, ten feet in front of her, a roadrunner rushes from one side of the road to the other.

"Beepbeep!" Marian cries, without even thinking.

When the phone rang, Hank was working in the kitchen. He put down his drill. "Go ahead, answer it," he said. "It might be the voice of Fate."

"Marian," the voice on the other end said, "I'm getting married."

"That's wonderful," Marian said. "Louise?"

"Who did you think it was?" Louise said. "Look, I want you to give me away."

"What?" Marian said.

"You're my last living connection to Daddy. It would say so much if you could stand in for him."

"Couldn't I just represent him in the audience?" Marian said.

"Come on, Mar," Louise said.

"What does your mother say?" Marian said.

"I don't care what she says," Louise said. "It's *my* wedding."

"I'm not sure I could handle it, Louise."

Listening in, Hank said, "Of course you could."

"Is someone there with you?" Louise said. "Your dark young friend?"

"It's Hank from across the street," Marian said. "You met him during the trial."

"No I didn't," Louise said. "You didn't introduce me to anyone."

"Surely I did," Marian said.

"Don't be defensive, Marian," Louise said. "It really doesn't matter. Anyway. Will you come?"

"I suppose so," Marian said.

"That's great," Louise said. "Wear anything you want. It's very informal. Bring your little friend."

After hanging up, she said to Hank, "I haven't even talked to her in *years*. Why on earth would she want me to give her away?"

"Maybe she loves you," Hank said.

"Maybe she just wants to bug her mother."

"Oh, come on," Hank said. "She's how old?"

"In her eighties somewhere," Marian said.

"I mean your stepdaughter," Hank said. "Isn't she a little old to be fighting with her mother?"

"You're never too old to fight with your mother," Marian said. She closed her eyes and saw herself striding down an aisle, hauling Louise by the wrist, Louise struggling to keep up. It *is* a sort of nice thing, she thought, a way to include Arthur on this day. Though surely the presence of Louise's mother—and the presence of Louise herself—would *imply* Arthur. Well, it would be interesting to see Louise again, after all this time. And what sort of man she was marrying.

"Sounds like a blast," Hank said.

"Come on, baby, come on." Williams is down on his belly in front of the rattlesnake, camera in one hand, a yellow stalk of dead grass in the other, pointing it toward the snake's nose. "Let's see some fang, babe."

Marian supposes in an emergency she could run to the nearest of the low white houses, though no sign of life is visible in any of them. A Mexican maid would probably answer the door. She imagines herself saying "Snake!" very loudly, enunciating clearly. "Rattle!" Shaking an imaginary baby rattle and then, at the woman's uncomprehending look, putting her palms together and waving her arms around, weaving her hips, trying to look serpentine. In college, a girl named Beth had told her she had just the right figure for belly dancing: *wide in the hips, thin and snaky on top.*

The maid would turn out to be the missus and would call back over her shoulder, into the dark cool depths of the tiled hall, "Harry! Another tourist got bit."

From the darkness a man's belly would emerge, followed by the man himself in a sleeveless undershirt, a soggy cigar hanging from his lip, his grizzled hair in a brush cut and his spectacles thicker than oil. "Where y'all from?" he'd gargle, and Marian would notice plastic tubes running from his nostrils to a tank that he pulled along beside him.

"Saratoga Springs," she'd say. "Please come." And she'd belly dance her way back through the housing development, the old fart gasping behind her, the wife scurrying along behind carrying the oxygen tank, to where Williams lay writhing on the ground, clutching his wrist above the spot where two gaping holes were rapidly disappearing into a bulbous swollen mass of flesh, and the villainous snake had slithered with silent satisfaction into the shade of a greasewood bush.

"Thanks, bud," Williams says. He gets to his knees, then to his feet. The snake is coiled up now, head raised, looking for all the world like a snake.

"Don't you think you're a little old to crawl around on the desert floor?" Marian says. Little bits of gravel and something sparkly like glass are embedded in the flesh of his elbows and knees.

"Never too old to grovel for my art, babe," he says.

Louise is also an artist, in a red-lipsticked, chain-smoking, brassy-haired way. She paints tiny, tiny little pictures, exquisite miniatures, on the heads of matches, the shafts of pine needles, anything so small Marian can see it only if she takes off her bifocals and holds it very close to her face.

"What's the point?" she asked Arthur once.

"Art needs no point," he'd explained in a voice that sounded very, very kind, but in fact was designed to make the interlocutor feel very, very stupid. He was tremendously defensive where His Girl was concerned.

And in fact Louise has achieved a certain degree of fame in what Marian believes is the art world. Once she and Arthur went to one of Louise's shows, where her works were displayed beneath magnifying glasses. People strolled from glass to glass, leaning over and producing positive-sounding murmurs. Once in a while they cried out and leaned closer to peer in.

"Are you sure this is the right road?" They have turned off the highway onto a secondary road, then onto a tertiary road, a track which is unpaved and so small it isn't even on the map Marian holds.

"Sure. I've been through here before." Williams has traveled around the area a number of times, though he has never stayed at The Back of Beyond, the inn where Louise will be getting married tomorrow.

"Why do you suppose Louise is having her wedding in the middle of nowhere?" Marian says.

"Lots of people get married there. You'll probably want to too, once you see it."

"I don't think so," Marian says. She likes the desert okay, but in small doses and for very short periods of time. She thinks Man in the Desert is like Man on the Moon, or Man On a Crowded Subway: All the preparation in the world is terrific as long as there is no accident. That For Which One Cannot Prepare.

They bump along. The vegetation has changed: there are tall yellow grasses and some yucca variants that are either just past or just about to bloom. Now and then they come to a wide flat puddle in the middle of the road. At the first one Williams stops, gets out of the car, and inches his way out into the middle of the water, where he looks right and left before coming back.

"What were you looking for?" Marian says.

"Flash floods," he says.

"In the desert?" She wonders if he's gotten too much sun.

"Absolutely," he says, driving the car very slowly through the puddle. "A wall of water can come on you so fast you don't know what hit you. *Never* step into one of those arroyos if there's even a *hint* of clouds."

"That was an arroyo?" Marian has begun to worry just a little about reaching the Back of Beyond in time for the wedding rehearsal, which is at four o'clock. She can't imagine why they are going this way. It isn't as if a sign had said *Scenic Viewpoint* or *Point of Interest*. There is no reason to be driving up this dirt road at midday under a killer sun.

When they come upon the stalled van, she immediately gets a bad feeling. Even under its coating of yellow dust, it's too bright to look at. Williams slows the little car and is just easing to the left to drive around the van when a man who has been underneath it scrambles to his feet, semaphoring his arms over his head to get their attention. His naked belly is streaked with grease and glistening with sweat. Williams stops the car.

"Don't get out," Marian whispers.

The man jogs around to Williams's side of the car and leans down. "Man am I glad to see you," he says, talking so fast Marian can hardly understand him. "Could you give me a jump? Because I can't get the engine started, could be the starter but there are other possibilities and I can't eliminate them. Can you jump me?"

"I don't have any cables," Williams says.

"I've got them. If you could pull your car up I can do all the work, I'm a mechanic but if you could just let me try them on your engine I think I could get it started. That's all it needs." The man wears no hat and no sunglasses, and the whites of his small, red-rimmed eyes stand out in his dark face. He doesn't look at Williams, but glances right and left, back and forth, as he speaks. Sweat streams down on either side of his nose into the gullies carved past his mouth, and drops of it fall from his chin.

"Sure," Williams says.

The man throws his hands up in an awkward gesture, of relief or perhaps victory, and jogs around the car to the back of his van. Fat joggles above the waistband of his slick green pants.

"I don't like this," Marian says in a low voice.

Williams shakes his head. "This is the desert, Mar. People can die."

The man is rummaging around in the dim interior of his van. When Marian lowers her sunglasses she can see inside; it's stuffed with boxes and piles of fabric and wadded newspapers and bottles and beat-up boots and coils of rope. A jar half-filled with black liquid stands on the ground beside the right rear tire. The man straightens up, waving the jumper cables. Williams backs and saws the car until it is nose to nose with the van, and reaches down to pop the hood.

"Jesus, Williams, that's the trunk." That's the last thing they need, to display their personal belongings to this guy. She opens her door and climbs out and the heat drops on her like a collapsing tent. She struggles through it to slam the trunk closed.

The man fixes the cables on the contact points and clambers into the driver's seat of the van, and Williams revs the engine. Marian trudges a little way up a rise beside the road, feeling as if she is barely moving. There are yellow sunflowery things blooming among the gray bunch grasses, and in the distance she can see a hint of mountains, faint and blurred at the end of the endless desert. The man is shouting at Williams through the noise of the engine and Williams is nodding as he sits in the car, his foot on the gas.

Marian wonders if she will know when they are about to die. The guy is probably a veteran, off drugs for now but way, way down on his luck, and nuts. He's probably done this before, pretending to have trouble with his van and then when his Samaritans' defenses are down he kills them. Buries them in the desert, takes their water, and drives merrily away. The little rented car will be found, but this clever guy will be long gone. No one will ever know what happened.

Marian and Williams will disappear without a trace.

Williams revs the engine when the man waves his hand, lets it slow when the man motions downward.

How do people get through life, she wonders. How on earth do you get through life with no money and no intelligence and no luck?

The van doesn't start. Marian sits on a rock watching the man run back and forth from the engine to the back of the van, hauling grease-blackened tools from soggy cardboard boxes. She winces as he drops to the ground and pushes himself under the car, no little wheeled dolly, not even a piece of cardboard between his flesh and the dirty gravel. He *must* be on drugs, she thinks, that he doesn't feel the gravel digging into his bare back.

Williams gets out of the car and goes over to look into the engine. "I don't think it's the battery," she hears him say. The guy must have said something from under the car because Williams says, "No, more like the alternator," at which the man's arms drop to the ground at his sides as if in defeat. He lies still for a moment, then digs his heels into the ground and drags himself out.

Holding a wrench, he gets up and walks over to stand beside Williams.

Move away from him, Marian thinks, her heart speeding. *Just slowly step away.*

Williams, having no instinct for self preservation, doesn't respond. Instead he leans forward and points at something under the hood. The man looks at the back of Williams's head for a long moment before he too leans forward to look.

Marian stands up and looks around again, but no car has appeared on the snake of road that lies like a mirage across the gray-green desert. Suppose the man does something to Williams. Or suppose Williams just keels over in the heat. They have one small bottle of water in the car which by now is probably hot enough to make tea. She would bathe Williams's face and wet his lips and drag him into the shade of the car; then what? Leave him with the man while she goes for help? Send the man for help? Sit companionably with the crazy man and wait to be found?

She would break off the rearview mirror and use it to flash signals at passing jets. She would break the mirror itself and flash it at the man if he should threaten her or Williams.

Williams walks over and reaches into the back seat of the car and brings out his camera bag. He takes the camera out of the case and fiddles with it, then walks back to where the man is still leaning into the engine. Williams says something and the man jerks his head up. Williams raises his hand as if to say *stay* and the man stays motionless. Williams steps back and raises the camera, and Marian sees the man's bright teeth. Williams leans over the engine and takes its picture, then walks around and takes a picture of the back of the van and the innards littering the ground.

He's a genius, Marian thinks. *Not an artist, but a genius.* She stands up and walks slowly back to the car.

"Anything," the man is saying. He doesn't look at her, but he doesn't look at Williams either, who stands with his arms folded against his chest and his camera in one hand as he listens to the man. The man looks at his own empty hand, at the right front tire of the rental car, at the hood of the van, propped open above the engine. "Give me enough time and the right tools and I can repair anything. I'm a skilled worker. You've heard of those Indians, those Mohawks, that do that highwire construction work, balancing on the edge of heights? I can do that with any kind of mechanical piece. If I have the right tools, you know? But the water here is polluted, chromium, toluene, you name it. Look at it." He gestures toward the jar of black water. "No way I would put that in my engine, you know?"

"Is that all the water you have?" Williams says. "You can't stay out here without water."

"A decent wrench would make the difference," the man says.

"Not without water," Williams says. "Look, I've been out here before. No one might come this way for weeks."

"We've got some," Marian says. She reaches into the back seat and pulls out the bottle of water she would have used to bathe Williams's fevered brow. It *is* warm. She holds it out to the man, who takes it without looking at her. "We could leave this with you. We don't need it."

Williams looks at her. "You know how long that would last, babe?"

"It's all we've *got*, Williams," she says.

Williams turns back to the man and says, "We'll take you into town."

"It could be I need a new alternator," he says. "It's been known to happen. If I just had the right tools I could get it running good enough to get me to town. Even a wrench."

"Look, lock up your van and we'll take you into town. You can load up on water and get what you need."

"I could get the wrench," the man says hopelessly, and he heads for the back of the van.

"Williams, we have to be there by four o'clock," Marian says.

"Marian, it's just the rehearsal." She sees him place an extremely patient look on his face. "We can't leave this guy out here."

Of course she knows that. People die in this heat, dozens of them every year. She's seen it in the papers; she's tried to imagine the desperation that drives people to leave what homes they know and cross the desert. When all that waits for even the luckiest is janitorial work and a hot apartment shared by twenty people.

Saving illegal Mexicans is one thing, but a serial killer?

The smell of the man's body oozes up and surrounds her, and with each bump and pothole the sharp, aggressive odor of his breath surges forward and curls around her head, right at nose level. She holds her sun hat over her nose and mouth. He talks nonstop for the two hours and eighteen minutes it takes to drive to Tucson, but he doesn't give them any information about himself, he doesn't ask anything about them, and he barely responds when Williams responds to him. After he ignores several of her remarks, Marian stops trying to be kind. The man is clearly disturbed, and there's no point in trying to pretend he isn't. They'll be lucky to get to Tucson alive.

But they do, and they spend another hour driving through the ugly, flat, traffic-ridden streets of Tucson's low rent outskirts, looking for Road Runner Auto Repair. By the time they find it, it has closed for the day, although it is only three o'clock. They stand helplessly before the crude but recognizable Roadrunner hand painted on the shop's glass door, the words *BeepBeep!* rising from its mouth in a little white balloon. Williams points out that lots of repair shops close early in the day, since they often start at godawful hours in the morning, and besides, it's Friday.

"And?" Marian says. She has the sudden feeling that Williams and the man are in cahoots. She has been with them all afternoon, all day, and they have never said anything that indicated any kind of conspiracy, but she feels that somehow they have made a secret agreement without her knowledge, as if men can communicate with grunts and gestures and odors that a woman knows nothing of.

But then the man says, "My sister." He throws his arm down, as if he were hurling a heavy tool to the ground. "I'm calling her!" he shouts, and he stomps over to yank the car door open. He leans in and takes something from the depths of the greasy bag he brought with him. They hear a series of tiny *beeps*.

Williams and Marian look at each other.

"A cell phone," she says.

Williams's face is lined and gray under the russet flush from the day's overdose of sunlight, and the whites of his eyes are red. He isn't as young as he used to be, and now he has spent all day trying to help a man in trouble. In *danger*. Marian is embarrassed at the thought of her grumpiness. She rolls her eyes and then smiles at him, hoping he understands she's mocking the troubled man and making light of the fact that they are about to miss the wedding rehearsal and in another hour they will start missing the rehearsal dinner.

"She's coming to get me." The man shouts as if they are a block away. As he comes toward them, Marian notices that he walks unsteadily. An inner ear problem, maybe. "She said, 'Oh, you're at the Road Runner, I'm on my way.' She doesn't want to know about me, but she does."

"Yeah, my family's like that," Williams says. "They don't want to know about me, either, but they can't help it."

"You can go now," the man says, waving the cell phone. "My sister's coming so you can go now."

"We can wait," Williams says pleasantly.

"No, no, no, you go," the man says. "I'm waiting for her." He looks over his shoulder, then moves sideways until he reaches the shop door, and he leans back on it so that for a moment the *BeepBeep!* balloon is rising right out of his head. Then he slides down and sits against the door with his knees drawn up, clutching the greasy bag and the cell phone to his chest. "I'm waiting," he says loudly.

"Really, it's no trouble," Marian says, but the man turns his face away.

"We'll wait till she comes," Williams says firmly.

The man closes his eyes and shakes his head. "No, no no no no." His voice rises with each *no*. "My sister's coming. You go *now*."

And so they drive off, leaving the man sitting in front of the Road Runner. Marian waves, but he doesn't wave back.

"Do you think he really has a sister?" she says.

"Well." Williams sighs. "I don't think he's capable of making her up."

The sun is still strong, but it's so low in the sky that the shadows of the buildings lie across the street; the car moves through a cool gray square of shade, then a hot patch of blinding light that shoots in at the side of Marian's sunglasses, then back into shadow again. Hot bright / cool gray / hot bright / cool gray.

"Strobe City," she says.

"Why is it always Something City with you?" Williams says.

She looks at him. This side of his face is untouched by the strobing of the sun.

"Why can't you say *The sun is making patterns on my eyes?* Instead you say *Strobe City* and I'm supposed to laugh."

"You're not supposed to laugh," she says. "I just said it. It doesn't mean anything."

"Don't you take anything seriously?"

"I take everything seriously," Marian says. "Ever since Arthur I can hardly even breathe."

"You think you're the only one?" He pulls into the parking lot of an abandoned strip mall and turns off the engine, and sits gripping the steering wheel. "I signed on too, you know. Late, maybe. But I'm here now."

In the middle of a dead and dry planting strip a white plastic shopping bag impaled on a prickly pear cactus is whipping madly in the wind. It whips and whips and gets nowhere.

Marian reaches over and takes Williams's hand. "For a long time I liked to think that I'd find happiness with someone." She closes her eyes. "I could see a big, rolling meadow with a copse of oaks at the far edge, and I could see myself walking out through tall grass and swaying seedheads to meet someone who was in it somewhere. Then I met Arthur, and for a long time I thought it was him."

"You were younger then," Williams says. "How could you even imagine me?"

They watch the dancing bag.

"Maybe we should go back and check on him," Marian says.

"That guy was scary," he says, frowning. "I can't believe we let him in our car."

"Well, what were we supposed to do?"

"Ask if he had a cell phone," Williams says. "Jesus, can you believe it?"

"You're the tech guy," she says. "Maybe you should sign us up for the twenty-first century."

He laughs and holds her hand to his lips. Then he starts up and they drive back to Road Runner Auto Repair.

The man isn't there, though. No sign of him. No sister, no cell phone, no serial killer. There is nothing to do but turn around and go on. They stop for burritos. Then, while Williams gases up, Marian uses an old fashioned pay phone to call The Back of Beyond.

"The missing stepmother!" cries the woman who answers the phone. "Are you all right, hon?"

Marian says she is. She tells the woman to tell Louise that she'll be there late tonight.

"She'll be tickled to hear it," the woman says. "But I think you're in trouble, sweetheart."

In the dim light of dusk the geography is transformed. As they drive away from the city the land swells up from the highway into little hills and cliffs, and as the road curves around a rise, tiny mountains materialize at the horizon, dark against the white-blue sky.

"What mountains are those?" Marian says. She looks over at Williams. He has fallen asleep, his head back against the headrest and his mouth open.

Tomorrow it will seem like such a non-emergency, a non-event! A man's car broke down and Williams and Marian took him back into town and dropped him off at a car repair shop.

"*Now* will you get a cell phone?" Louise will say.

But for tonight they're safe. All the way to the Back of Beyond, Marian thinks of the man's sweaty, dirty skin and smells the sickening odor of his breath. She imagines what would have happened if she and Williams hadn't stopped. She pictures the man's body, desiccated and stark and torn, the turkey vultures beadily snacking away. She sees the old van, bleached and sandblasted, standing in the desert forever, all those papers and tools and greasy rags scattered across the sand.

That American dream, Marian thinks. People think you can just pack up and go. Just go, and leave it all behind.

Robert Parham

March

Great light, sudden and short,
that pretends to be April.

We know the liar, of course,
by the way he whistles,

as the clouds scud as if
to flee, and the eaves

call out "Pretender!"
Further south, though, birds

begin to turn their heads
back, as if pulled toward

where they have been, sun
on the invisible compass,

buds on the dogwood stems
so small they seem a dew,

remnant, yet to be shaken
by the movement of those

asleep with uneasy dreams
that all involve returning.

Brandon Krieg

Prodigal

I remember as a child the river alien cutting cold
through the whirlwind of hot dust
picking clean the cliffs' ribs,

cliffs against which
the dam builders and their families camped
an unimproved people—
my father and the other welders in black hood and leathers,
dressed otherwise as Job,

and I made to sit with the brutal women in
the hot whirlwind, my finger
on a psalm without
pulse.

The river shone otherworldly swift—I thought it
began on a peak above the clouds
among the eagles on coins
mercifully cold
though my eyes found no rest in the glare of it
and I was forbidden to go near it.

I fell from a corrugated pipe
while trying to see into it
and it sucked the dust from my mouth
and it cased me in a tone like that of a suspended I-beam
that has clipped concrete and scintillates aloud.

I would not come out into the dust again;
I would stay overawed.

But by the coffer dam the Army Corps raised me up
and the men gathered around their dripping prodigal
and I mocked them with the psalm's still waters.

Squaw Fish

My greatest luck seemed the three-dollar bounty
on the squaw fish that year, that preys
on salmon smolts and has the fine bones woven
tightly into its flesh: sure mark of a trash fish.

It has a puckered suckermouth, slimy spade-shaped
scales, and a bald gold eye that begs you to smash it.
I would not even remove a small one from my line
but would swing it from the water

like a lantern on a chain, dashing its light out
on the rocks, sometimes finding gold pieces
of eye on the rocks the next day.
It inspired cruelty in me I explained to David

my younger brother was mercy—"Put them out
of their dumb misery." He came to love those
times when mercy was required of him, acting
like a rush of water that cannot help itself

when the new channel is cut. The summer before he left
for the war we fished every evening and caught
ten thousand dollars worth between us and bought
a drift boat to take down the Rogue in spring.

Brandon Krieg

I have not made a cast since his death. The boat is adrift
on the side of my house and sometimes fills with rain.
I come to sit where we fished to be sure he is not
casting in the eyes that cover the rocks in my dream.

Inversion Among the Fish Counters at Bonneville Dam

I could count seven hundred salmon flashes in an hour
while watching in the falling wall of water
the triumph of Caesar, red as Capitoline Jupiter

not long before he was murdered and deified. Some still leave,
it's said, flowers in the forum where his tomb is thought to be.
Nevermind. I was a classics major home from the University

with a nervous disorder, and was told a repetitive task
might take my mind off Rome's decline. I sat before a glass
viewing window and counted, in their spawning masks—

hook-jawed, severe—male Chinook returning.
Joe Garrison sat in the other folding chair, burning
as he said, his Indian half with a flask, and earning

nearly twice my wage for the more difficult-to-spot hens.
"What's your other half, Joe?" I asked. "Half salmon,"
he said, "what's yours?" I said: "Half Imperial Roman."

He laughed. "The best gladiators were Colville Indians," he said,
"They learned by spearing salmon to spear a man dead
at thirty yards from a speeding El Camino's bed."

I laughed hard. Then wanting to reach him these words
formed by inversion before I could check them. We both heard:
"To kill a man, kill his salmon—that's what the Romans learned."

Perhaps a hundred fish flashed by before he spoke.
I couldn't count a single one. He stood up. "My heart just broke,"
he said and left his post. Was he serious? I couldn't look.

Peter Harris

Whitman's Widow in Springtime

I was the eldest, pale from excellence; my necklace
strung with momma/poppa shoulds and musts.
Winters, I'd watch the sun attempt to flood
the dooryard, and then slide back.

I'd just turned 28 the day he saw me
behind my bedroom lace. He coaxed me out,
said the world is too immense for death by etiquette.
He bought me earthen oils, stretched me canvases.

I shocked us both by painting a butterfly vagina
tangled in spider lilies, a volcanic flame all flecked
with dark-winged seeds, sheathed in a moist green core.
He watched me paint it. rising like a magic beanstalk,

tendrilling that melancholic in the moon.
I crooned, *I'll be your Jesus knuckle, your dowsing stick,*
your wild adept. I'll ride the midnight tiger
bareback, standing up, eyes shut.

That spring, when I foretold that oaks would swim,
that pickerel would suture all the daffodils, he fell
for me; put down his pen. We married on the sly.
I knew Walt's ways. Yet who was he but love?

He showed me how to enter heaven through a slit,
make myself corona when I speechify.

Peter Harris

Helped me love the men who carried him away.
April's here again. Walt's gone,

but the brush he bought brims full of lip.
I'll paint your face wild rhubarb, pry apart
the clouds in that storm sky that you haul around.
Abide, I'll help your tongue leap like a trout.

Alamgir Hashmi

Earthworms

Those crawly things, the slime?

Razzle of random falling
rain in sectors the forecast failed.
That is monsoon.

But the earth has formed them,
nurtured for this day,
released.

Off with your wellingtons,
let them go.
Smell the earth's moisture.

They slither, slide, copulate, or recoil
from any outline drawn here,
assuming life, and hardly know.

Brian Shawver

Ostriches

THE STANDARD PROCEDURE IS, you touch their foreheads with an electric stunner, then hang them up with chains, inverted, and slash their necks. The way they kill cattle. It's hard to imagine it working very well—their heads bob around so much I can't see how you'd get a clean shot. Although if you did manage to stun them, it would be easy to cut the jugular, those things must be as long as jump ropes.

Anyway, it was beside the point on Kathy's farm, as she couldn't afford a stunner—two thousand for a used one, while Kath barely had enough to renew the subscription for the magazine they were advertised in. So "you'll find a way, honey bear, you'll find a way," is what she said to me on the drive out west, and at that point I'd already cashed in some of my retirement and lied about the fictional death of a fictional brother in order to get a hardship leave from the high school where I taught Spanish and health. Slaughtering a few birds didn't seem like much on top of that.

Surly, surly beasts they are. No surprise there. In the animal kingdom, it's always the half-cute, half-ugly ones that have difficult personalities— camels, mules, pugs. It's surprising they're still a species at all. You'd think over the years the murderous rage they engender would have caught up with them. I wonder if their main Darwinian advantage is that they're such big awkward things—no matter how bad you want to kill them, by the time you've figured out how to do it, you've settled down a little.

Kathy first told me about them in a Red Roof Inn off a Kansas City interstate. She showed me pamphlets and pie charts and something called a flow graph. It might have been impressive in an office building or some-place, but almost everything loses its authority in a Kansas City motel room, plus she wasn't wearing any pants.

Afterwards, I said, "Whoa, are you asking for money?"

"Not money, help."

"I don't know what kind of help I can give, sweet stuff. I don't believe I've ever even met an ostrich. I sure didn't know you could eat them."

"Well you can. I just showed you."

Mostly she'd shown me that a few thousand people in California ate them, and that some speculators thought the trend would spread east-ward. She'd told me there were three times as many ostrich farms in Kansas as there had been just a year ago. I told her I had three times as many boobies as I had this morning, and she gave me a look that was all annoyance, like I was a kindergarten class laughing at a fart.

"Where'd you get the money?" I said.

"Oh, you don't want to know."

"You're probably right," I said, kind of ironically, but she nodded as if I'd made a wise decision. Kathy was the kind of girl who just stumbled into bizarre fortunes, nothing that set her up very well, just things that changed her life oddly and temporarily. She was the kind of girl who won pink Cadillacs in poker games, who got flown to Rio by dirty old men. And apparently she was the kind of girl who came into possession of an ostrich ranch outside of Goodland, Kansas, a six hour drive from where we were sitting on I-70.

I say all this like I knew her well, but I didn't. At that point, I'd known her for twenty-eight days. You can cram a lot of knowing into that span, but we hadn't done that. We'd been mostly on our own, working our jobs, living our lives. She might have been seeing other men. In those days, there had probably been fifty to sixty hours of actually me-and-Kathy contact. Enough to have some sex, to hear some stories, to tell some lies you'll have to straighten out later, to come to an unarticulated decision about the lengths you'll go to in order to keep this woman in your life.

Along with the ranch and the two dozen birds, Kath had inherited a young hippie named Deke who would work with me in the pens while she tended to the books and applied for Department of Agriculture grants. When I say he was a hippie I don't mean he wore tie-dyes and played bongos, I just mean he smelled bad and kept his eyes half-closed and wore a smile that said he was a little too pleased with how mellow he was. Also, he had long, unwashed hair that he continually tried to nurture into dread locks, but it never quite took. He didn't have the genes for it, he told me once. I got the sense this was one of the great disappointments of his life.

On the first day Deke showed me how to muck the stalls—the birds crap like horses—which turned out to be my main job, since feeding them was a complicated process. Deke mixed corn and seed and flax, tailoring the proportions for each bird, and often he had to coax them into eating, as if they were toddlers; he'd pretend to gobble a handful of meal himself or he'd spray the stuff with sugar water. It was sad to see, the way they took advantage of Deke. But that's the way with ostriches, you give them an inch and soon you're wiping their asses for them.

On my third day Deke asked if I wanted to see something and I said yes please. I wanted out of there in a bad way. The barn was dark and noisy and smelly, like the monkey house in a poorly funded zoo. I'd started wearing a wet bandana over my face and the night before I'd woken up four times to blow the dust and stink out of my nostrils. I kept thinking about how I was supposed to be in a basement classroom at Raymore High School, 320 miles to the west, talking about the pluperfect or chlamydia. That didn't strike me as a very desirable place to be either, but if you were going to not be there, surely you could come up with a better alternative than this.

Deke told me to wait outside, and soon he came out with two birds, a female named Hettie and a male named Jake. He had them on string leashes. The birds weren't resisting, just jutting along like they do, like their bones have been taken out and put together in the wrong order.

"You're not going to believe this, mijo." Ever since I told him I taught Spanish, he'd called me mijo. It didn't make any sense, but I like having nicknames.

He wrestled the birds into position—he wasn't afraid to handle them, I'll give that to Deke—and soon had them both facing west. There was a short rise in the distance, and then nothing beyond that until you hit the Rocky Mountains. Each bird was tethered at the neck to a spool of kite string. Deke pulled a red firecracker out of his back pocket, the fat kind the janitors are occasionally finding in toilets at the high school. He lit it, dropped it to the ground, and when it exploded the birds shot off toward Colorado.

"Holy shit," I said.

"I know," said Deke, in the near-falsetto of the stoned. "Fucking incredible, yeah?"

"I had no idea."

"Fastest birds in the world. Almost as fast as quarter horses. They race them in the Middle East."

They'd gone over a hundred yards in the time it took us to have this conversation. Deke was fidgeting with the kite string now, trying to gauge the slack, so that it wouldn't snap when they reached the end. It worked with Hettie; she felt the tension and slowed. But the maneuver took too long, and by the time Deke turned to Jake's spool the extra string was almost gone. Then the line went slack. Jake kept on going, over the rise, with a few dozen feet of kite string hanging off his neck.

"Whoops," said Deke.

"Think she'll notice?" I said.

He didn't say anything, just stared off at Jake's ever-shrinking behind.

"Deke," I said a few times, until he looked at me. I raised my eyebrows in a way that shed responsibility, as if to say I was the sane one here, the one who couldn't possibly have released an ostrich onto the prairie. "Someone will find him, right?"

"Yeah, maybe," he said finally, with a self-conscious quality of awe in his voice. "There are farms that direction. Someone fixing an irrigator maybe."

"Or he might cross Route Nine. Someone could drive along and see him."

"Yeah, that too. Some dude just driving along, just happens to see Jake tearing at him out of nowhere."

"Yeah, yeah, that could happen."

"I'll tell you this," Deke said. "I'd give anything to be that dude."

She'd brought up the killing on the drive out west. That was when she told me about the stunners, and how she couldn't afford one, and how she was sure I'd figure something out. But she didn't bring it up again until after the first week. There were lots of intimate moments in that week, us getting to know each other just as much as we were getting to know all the other new stuff: the new bed, the new house, the new weather and accents you encounter in that part of the state. In Kansas City, we'd mostly made love in cars and motels, due to our complex room-mate situations. And all of a sudden we're playing house in a western Kansas farmstead. It was mostly strange at night: brush your teeth, set the alarm, lay there wondering how to signify your desire, not being too upset if it's not reciprocated. Not that I lost interest—we had probably eight or nine good screws in that first week—I'm just saying it's different to sleep with a woman when you know that afterwards you'll lay beside her all night, that she'll smell your midnight farts.

On Tuesday during the second week, Kath visited the pens. We were hauling feed sacks, and she gave a cough to call attention to herself, like she'd caught us in the middle of doing something awkward.

"There's my hard-working boys."

"Yep," I said. "There's us."

"Feeding the birds?"

Deke said "Yup" very quickly, to stake the claim on the chore. Sometimes he was less easy-going than you'd expect a hippie to be, and he took every chance to point out that feeding was his job, and not even Kath had the right to offer advice about it.

"We need to talk about harvesting," Kath said. She dropped the "g" on "harvesting." Her accent got a little more country every day, as did her outfits—right now she had on jeans and a denim shirt with the sleeves cut off. In Kansas City, she wouldn't have worn it to get the mail.

"Harvesting."

"That's the word the books use. Call it what you want. But we got to get ten carcasses to Colby by Saturday. That's the deal. Louise and Ron-Ron we'll keep as breeders, they're the only ones who are up to it, according to the records."

Kath had an arrangement with a concern in Colby that would take delivery of the corpses, dress them, and store them in freezers until we found a distributor. She'd ordered another dozen live birds to be shipped out from Hays next Thursday. These ones were getting old, or hadn't been the reproducing type to begin with. Or maybe ostrich meat is only good when it's harvested at a certain age. I didn't know much.

"I've been thinking about those Colby people," I said. "They're going to be gutting them and filleting them and what-not, why don't they just do the killing too? It doesn't seem like much more to ask."

"Permits," she said. "You need a different kind of permit to kill animals on your property." It sounded true enough, but I could tell she didn't know it for sure.

"All right then," I said. "I guess Deke and I need to figure something out. You don't seem too keen on offering suggestions."

"Deke's taking the rest of the week off. He's a Buddhist."

"Oh. Is it some kind of Buddhist holiday?"

Deke laughed. He was squatting by the side of the barn, weeding out his little herb garden. He was always doing something like that, finding busy work when others were chatting or loafing. He didn't have an ounce of lazy in him, another reason it was hard to buy the hippie act.

"Something funny Deke?"

"We don't have holidays, Lester. I can't be in a place where animals are killed. I need to come back after purifying spirits have entered. It'll take three days, minimum."

"I've never heard that before, Deke. What kind of Buddhism is that?"

"The only kind, man," he said, under his breath, like he was talking to the basil.

"You agreed to do it, Lester," said Kath.

It was true, but I couldn't tell how that mattered. Back then, back when she said I'd find a way, everything was sunny and open-spaced, and only two hours earlier we'd performed reciprocal oral sex in a Salina motel. In the past week I'd spent more time with the ostriches than I had with her. I didn't like them much, but still, time spent together is hard to argue with. That favor of hers had put on weight.

"So how do I do it, Kath? You want me to do this, okay. But you got to tell me what you have in mind. You want me to drown the poor fuckers?"

"No Lester, that won't work. Everyone knows that."

"How then?"

"Shit, Lester. How complicated is it?"

Deke stood up, feeling either offended or morally compromised. He stomped off toward the farmhouse, where he had a room in the basement, with the stride and the expression of a teenager who's just been grounded.

"It's two thousand dollars down the tubes if they come out here and they don't have birds to collect. We have a contract."

She was looking off to the west, squinting, not selling it very hard, not bothering to look pretty or loving, not using any endearments. She said it for form's sake; it would have been embarrassing for me if she didn't at least pretend she had to argue me into it. But how did she know? Where does the arrogance come from, the kind it takes to ask a favor like that and know it'll be granted? Did she just assume she was pretty enough, or good enough in the sack, to haul me out to western Kansas and hand me this bizarre task and know I'd do it in the end? Or was it something particular she saw in me—a neediness, a possessiveness that practically begged her to give me such a challenge? A need to prove the lengths to which I would go for a gorgeous woman, for love, for something new in my life.

Last fall the school's drama kids performed *Much Ado About Nothing.* I don't remember the characters' names but I remember the kids who played them. In one scene Andrew Wynn, a popular black kid, declared his love for Lottie Jackson, a stunning little sophomore who had the gumption to try a British accent, even though it made her sound like something from the *Muppets.* Andrew told Lottie to send him on a mission to prove his love—anything, he said, absolutely anything. Right away she told him to kill his best friend. Right away Andrew said no. In fact he said, "not for the wide world." Those are the words I remember. But because Andrew Wynn is a pretty astute young thespian, and because Lottie looks the way she does, you could tell that no matter how good and true the refusal felt coming off his character's tongue—not for the wide world!—you also knew that he didn't have much choice in the end.

Glynnis would be first to go, no question about it. All ostriches are frustrating to look at, because of the way both halves of their bills naturally come together to create a constant little smirk; the expression is uncannily similar to the way certain of my students look when they're handed tardy slips. But Glynnis put a real attitude behind it, and you could never entirely convince yourself it was just the way evolution had decided to assemble her. If she could talk, I decided early on, she would sound exactly like the women from the school cafeteria, the ones who smoke cigarettes in the back hallway and dare you with their eyes to report them, the ones who, I'm convinced, have more than once spit into the taco meat out of pure spite. With people like the lunch ladies, and with animals like Glynnis, you can't help but blame them for their ugliness, to see a causal connection between their meanness and their hairy moles, their globby necks.

To be sure, all the birds were ornery. They all spit and kicked at me when I got near, and the racket in the barn was so constant and grating it was like they'd organized some sort of hissing schedule. Glynnis was the worst, though. Just full of hate. Often when I came around she couldn't decide whether to hiss or kick or spit or squawk, and she'd wind up doing all of it at once, which was such a dramatic display it scared or awed the others into silence. Glynnis was the kind of ostrich that other ostriches would admire, if they had the capacity.

None of this is to say I was eager to kill her. I thought about it rationally most of the time, in my moments away from the barn, as I watched the meager offerings from the Colby TV station with Kath leaned up against me, or during my long runs on the rural route, when I always aimed toward Colorado and returned a little disappointed that I hadn't seen Jake, the bird who'd broken from his string. In those moments I understood Glynnis was no more capable of considering my feelings than I was of laying a three-pound egg or digesting sand. It wasn't her fault. But one of them had to go first, and it wasn't a hard decision to make.

I woke up early on the first morning of Deke's vacation and began to gather the kind of things you might want to have handy if you planned to kill a person. In the farmhouse I collected a butcher knife, rat poison, and a Costco bottle of Tylenol with codeine. In the garage I found some rope and a baseball bat.

When I stomped into the barn, laden with weapons, the birds raised a chorus of screeching and hissing more intense than ever before. Animals know, of course, when you've got murder in the eye.

Glynnis shared a pen with Louise, the one who was going to be kept for breeding. When I opened the hatch door Louise turned to the corner and began pissing, while Glynnis bolted out of the opening and broke to the left. The barn had doors on both ends, and I'd made them secure, but for a while I wondered if she planned to crash on through. She pulled up just short of it, braking with a suddenness almost as surprising as her speed, and turned to me, cornered. I had the baseball bat cocked, the knife tucked into a belt loop, the bottle of codeine in my pocket, a snarl on my face. Out of instinct and fear I swung the bat and she dodged her shivering head—they tremble all the time, those birds, the way Katherine Hepburn did toward the end—but she dodged unluckily, and the bat connected.

Now there was blood on her face, rich and dark, just like ours, and she'd stopped moving, but she hadn't fallen. She stared straight ahead into nothing. It was unsettling, seeing her like that, placid and vacant, where before she'd always raised such a stink about her lot in life. I pushed the round bulk of her body to see what would happen. Nothing. She didn't resist, didn't fall. I pushed harder. She toppled onto her side, with her long puckered legs sticking straight out, but she wasn't dead.

I could have cut her throat. She was stunned exactly the way she was supposed to be, exactly the way the two thousand dollar stunners did it. I could even string her up with a chain, so that the blood could drain out and not soak the meat. The way they kill cattle. Then I could take a trip up and down the aisle, battering their brainless heads with ease and swagger. If I could kill Glynnis I could kill them all. How pleased Kathy would be, and how pleasingly unsettled, to find that I could do this for her, to learn that she had such a dangerous, efficient slayer of birds at her disposal.

But instead of cutting Glynnis, I grabbed her by the thighs and dragged her over to the drinking trough, which was wide and deep because it had to accommodate all of them. I lifted her round body—she made the noise that a sleeping child makes when it's picked up by its father, resisting with an endearing weakness—and I splashed her into the water. Then I tipped in the stereo that was on the tack ledge, a portable thing, the kind that used to be called a ghetto blaster. It hit the surface with a sinister sizzle. Yellow smoke belched out from the trough, as if I'd lit firecrackers there, and the wet black body of Glynnis shuddered with a new urgency, then was still.

The other birds began to squawk and hiss. They didn't like the smell, and neither did I. I unplugged the stereo and pulled it from the water by its cord. There was no shame in this, I thought. It was true I had been too squeamish, too cowardly, too childish to kill her the right way, but I had killed her nevertheless, and that was something. That was what I was supposed to do.

Only then did I realize the bird was probably ruined. Electrocution was not a proper way to slaughter animals. The flesh would be charred, the organs poisoned, or else there was just something unwholesome, unpalatable, about the way she had died. I wouldn't have wanted to eat her, I knew that. We would have to bury Glynnis now, I supposed, and of course it would be my job. I could picture the three of us standing over a burial mound in the back pasture, Deke chanting Zen funeral mantras, me standing solemn and sweaty, grave dirt sweat-stuck to my face. And Kath eyeing me the way she would from here on out, a look of exasperation and curiosity, a what-the-hell-was-he-thinking look but also a shade of pity in there, an acknowledgement of her responsibility for me. Her wish was my command. It was a big weight to carry, for both of us.

I hauled Glynnis out of the trough and laid her on the dusty ground. Wet and limp like that, she looked like an exaggerated version of a newly hatched bird—a sparrow, a robin—that had fallen out of its nest. The kind of thing your dog lays at your feet, thinking it's a present.

Did I have a future here? Would she kick me out after this, out of her bed, out of her barn? Perhaps. I had other options, ways to salvage some pride. I could drive back home in the Volvo, she wouldn't miss it much. First I could make a sign and tape it to Glynnis' carcass—Here's Your

Dead Bird Kath or Zen This Deke! or Fried Chicken, Help Yourself!—to show I was my own man. What I wanted, though, was to stay and raise the birds with Kath and Deke and to never kill them or watch them be killed, to live in the farmhouse like a weird hippie threesome and oversee an exponentially expanding community of ostriches. We would have to build other barns, hire new workers, put up fences to prevent escape. We could have races, like they did in the Middle East. It was a pleasing scenario to me, although of course the birds aren't worth much if you don't kill them, so the dream was too unlikely, even for a dream, to sustain.

The reality was I had been on the ranch for ten days, and I hadn't done too well. From Kath's standpoint, maybe I wasn't a total mess. There had been some good tumbles in the bedroom, and I'd pulled off a very tricky tostada casserole recipe the night before. I'd made her laugh at least one time every day, although there was a kind of failure in the fact that I kept track. But if you considered things from the ostriches' perspective, if you thought about how they might regard me, then there wasn't much to show for my tenure. One bird dead at my feet, another sprinting toward Denver on the open prairie, ten more staring befuddled from their pens, waiting for my rough hands.

Naton Leslie

And Bring Your Lover

You can feel the magic of bright nights...
all year long—Forest Park brochure

Forest Park is magical to the tune
of half a million bulbs fired up
for the holiday about winter birth,
but I am drafted into creating

a festival for spring death, Mardi Gras.
I'm assigned to hanging airy plastic
chains of thespian masks, or balloons cheeked
at the brass tip of a tank I truck there.

Memories are ready to be made. But
sham finery undermines all my will,
my cotton good humor crushed in the night.
I decide to not attend, to ignore

the delights turned on, off in my body
for the ever-pending demise of God.

Naton Leslie

Emlenton Outfitters

Overnight Trips for Hunting and Fishing—brochure

My family took the old two-lane
from Ohio past Emlenton, Pennsylvania,
headlong down to the river, a hill
as steep as a string of dropped promises,
the longest enroute to my father's home,
the passage over the river a great
remembering instead. I loved

the heart-rushing plunge, neck-craning
hairpins. Traveled for two centuries,
the road was graveled with heroics,
and the iron bridge at bottom
was the reward, the Allegheny slipping
under like the broad bands of time,
the mental schematic I carried
of the decades, width linked
to what I knew had happened then,
the 1860s fat with civil war,
and the 1930s with railyards,
long lines and my father's memories.

But the interstate tamed the route
back to his storied hills. A concrete
span portaged us across mountain tops,
airborne, the overlooked Emlenton
now off-route, a moment of clearing
around the now thin, thin river.

Robert E. Wood

Castello di Gorizia

bastion of medieval mediocrity
emboldens
poets longing for unmerited
longevity.
Words are painted on the stones
by the trebuchet—
an installation.
I am tempted there
to leave behind these words
that fall like stones
though from no great height.

Robert E. Wood

Water Music

across cobblestones
tin percussion
on the hoods and roofs of cars
water streaming from awnings
pooling
water dropping from eaves
tires sibilant over the street
laughter of girls racing home wet
silence
hammer on stone
birdsong, church bells
thunder announcing the next movement.

Martina Nicholson

Dancing Together

Even if the candle burns out
We will still be dancing together:
Gliding through the magic round about,
You and I are made for stormy weather.

We will still be dancing together,
Long after the stars are gone—
You and I are made for stormy weather,
Running through the rain on the lawn.

Long after the stars are gone,
What has been true for me will be you:
Running through the rain on the lawn,
Every memory holds the golden clue.

What has been true for me will be you:
Gliding through the magic round about,
Every memory holds the golden clue,
Even if the candle burns out.

Jerah Chadwick

SONG: *Tohono O'Odam Basket*

—for Will Inman

Gray-green bands of yucca define
the way of bleached grass extending
from his feet, this man stitched in
Devil's Claw black entering
the maze of desert colors.

I'itoi, Tohono O'Odam call him
Elder Brother, and weave the story
of his wandering through the changing
pattern of a land where all paths lead
back to self, to center. Look the damp

spot of your shadow too
dries as you reach it, a trail
going on because you follow
in this labyrinth of light
everywhere guides us home.

Mark Spitzer

State Record Gar

IT WAS ONE OF THOSE totally humid, hundred-degree, early August Arkansas days, now cooling down in the amber evening. My wife and I were out on our lake, which is more like a Southern swamp. Lake Conway has an average depth of six feet and is full of water moccasins, herons, ducks, turtles, and big old ugly fish. The other day, a talkative guy at the bait store told me he'd been catching catfish at night by just hanging out in the boat lanes which cut through the cypress stumps. So that's where we were at sunset, in the deepest boat lane out there, hovering above a long gone serpentine pond known as Gold Lake, which disappeared in the forties when the Corps of Engineers put up the dam to create the largest game and fish commission lake in the country.

There was a slight breeze, keeping the mosquitoes off. Robin caught a small blue and we threw it back. She was fishing with her girly pink rod, and I had two lines out: a nightcrawler on my medium-weight spincasting rod, and a liver on my heavy-duty catfishing rod.

An occasional fish slapped the surface and the bats were just beginning to flash. It was getting hard to see, so when I couldn't spot my huge-ass bobber, I figured it was just the dusk. Still, my other was visible, so maybe a catfish came along and took it under. Usually, though, when a cat strikes, the float reappears pretty quickly. This float, however, wasn't coming up.

What the hell, I figured, and cranked back, setting the hook. The rod immediately bowed and I felt the weight on the other end. But it wasn't the weight of some casual flathead just nosing along on the bottom—it was the weight of something moving fast. Something that had struck my liver like a missile and was making its getaway.

So I horsed it in and horsed it in, and then we saw it: a big thick silvery gar, which immediately changed its course the moment we saw it and it saw us. It was parallel to the canoe, seven feet away from us, shooting for the bow, and cutting across my other line.

Robin grabbed the net and I cranked back on my rod again. The gar started flapping all over and kicking up a ruckus, but I managed to get it right beneath me. Then leading it back toward the stern, I turned it around and hauled it forward again, right across my other line again—toward the net, which was two feet in diameter. The three-foot gar refused to go in.

I had no choice but to try again. Leading it back to the rear of the boat, it splashed me a good one in the face, but I got it switched around, then led it head-first into the net. Robin scooped it up and dropped it in the boat between us, where it proceeded to smack around like no fish I'd ever caught. It was knocking my gear all over the place, and I practically had to tackle it to keep it in the boat.

After a few minutes, though, I cut away all the lines it was tangled in, then got it unwrapped from the net. But as soon as I got all that stuff out of the way, it went berserk again. Until I grabbed it, pinned it with one hand, and worked the treble hook out of the flesh underneath its jaw.

"It's a spotted gar," I told Robin, "a seven-pounder."

I could tell by imagining its length divided into seven separate one-pound slaps of hamburger. But to make sure, I weaseled a stringer through an armored gill and out its fanged gator-mouth, then hooked that stringer to the hand-held scale. Yep, seven pounds!

"Let's let it go," Robin suggested, because we already had tons of gar meat in the fridge.

I agreed. These days, I only keep those that drown on my droplines. If their eyes are still clear, that is, and they haven't been shredded by the turtles.

Still, we discussed the fact that it could be a state record, which would mean keeping it overnight, then taking it to the Post Office in the morning, where I'd have to wait for a Game & Fish agent to weigh it on a certified scale, then sign the appropriate paperwork. According to the minnow guy at Bate's Baits in Mayflower, the angler who caught the state-record buffalo had to wait five hours for an agent to meet him last summer, and when that agent finally arrived, his fish was dead and weighed less.

I'd just read a week ago that the state record was eleven pounds two ounces—according to a tourist pamphlet we'd picked up while driving through the Arkansas wine country. It was a glossy chamber-of-commerce publication that encouraged consumers to get back to nature via jet skis and ATVs. I should've known better than to trust that stupid thing!

Anyway, we admired the gar twisting in my grip. It was long and proud, more silvery than spotty, but the spots could be made out on its head. It wasn't huge like an alligator gar, but it was pretty dang jumbo for its species.

"Will it be alright?" Robin asked.

"Sure," I said.

Robin took a picture. She thought the flash didn't go off, but I thought it did.

Then unstringing it, I lowered it into the lake and held it by the base of its tail. It began to sink, and then it kicked. It didn't have the strength to break away, but I figured that the snap I just witnessed meant it had some life left in it. So I let it go, then watched it spiral straight down. Its tail never moved, the murk consumed it, and I found myself cringing when I felt it settle on the bottom, slack and languid, with no will or strength to get up at all.

Back at the ranch, I Googled "spotted gar" and "Arkansas" and "state record," only to find out what I suspected. The state record for rod and reel was six pounds twelve ounces. That eleven pounder was taken with a bow and arrow.

"AAAAAAARGH!", of course, was my first reaction. Like an idiot, I'd let it get away.

My second reaction was to email my friend Keith "Catfish" Sutton, who's a local wildlife writer, about what a moron I had been. He emailed me back instantly and advised going back and trying to find it, because

Blurry photo of author with unofficial Arkansas state-record spotted gar.

back when he had been the record keeper for Arkansas Game & Fish, a guy had called him up after releasing some sort of whopper trout. That guy told Catfish what the trout weighed, and Catfish told the guy that it could've been the state record. So the guy went back to the dock where he'd released it and went poking around with a broomstick. Miraculously, he managed to skewer the injured fish through the gills, and he got it back. Still, there was no category for catching a fish with a broom, but he got a witness to sign an affidavit that he caught it the first time on rod and reel, and then he wasn't shit out of luck.

Catfish also told me about how he and a buddy once went fishing in some pond and his friend caught a two-pound spotted gar. Back then, this fish didn't even merit a listing in the Arkansas record books, so Catfish encouraged the guy to take his in. The guy did, he got the official state record, but it didn't last long.

These stories, however, were little consolation. I had caught the unofficial state record spotted gar, but only two people in the world would ever really know for sure. But even worse, I couldn't get the image out of my mind of its motionless tail sinking in the lake, where the ding-dang turtles had been raping my bait all summer long.

I'd recently seen a show on TV about the pains taken to release a baby great white shark. The doctors and biologists who transferred it from tank to stretcher were scrambling to keep it alive. They shoved oxygen tubes into its gills, because if sharks can't swim, sharks can't breathe. The biggest danger they were facing was that it could've gone into cardiac arrest.

So I couldn't help wondering if I'd given that gar a heart attack. Or maybe it was so old that it might've just pooped out, like that world-record blue cat caught in Illinois a few years back. After being manhandled by its captor to get the trophy shot, then held in a bathtub, then moved to a truck, its delicate organs couldn't take the pressure, since they're basically used to zero gravity deep down in the Mississippi. That 124-pound catfish died en route to the Cabella's in Kansas City, where it'd been destined to amuse customers for the rest of its aquarium life.

At least the guy who caught that cat knew he murdered it. I, on the other hand, would never know what became of my gar. And since there's sixty-three miles of shoreline on Lake Conway, and 67,000 acres of silt and weeds and muck under that, and since the turtles had probably found it by now, I knew that going back with a broom and poking around wasn't gonna do jack.

Inevitably, I made it my mission to re-catch that gar. Or catch one of his pals, since I figured there were others out there close to the same size. I'd recently seen some big ones scattered on the shore, thanks to the "conservation efforts" of local bowhunters who think they're doing the environment a service by killing gar willy-nilly, then leaving their corpses for the flies. Some of these were longnose, but most of them were spotted gar, with a few shortnose thrown into the mix.

My friend the legendary Rex Rose was coming up from Florida, so I figured I'd enlist him in my drama. Robin likes fishing occasionally, but not when I get obsessive and go for gar every day—which is what I'd been doing every night for the last four nights, having launched an all-out Megalomaniac Monsterquest to get my name in the record book. Because Dangnabbit, I already caught that fish, so I deserved it!

What I neglected to remind myself of, though, was that Rex had already broken my other canoe—the Lümpenkraft—twice. Once in Louisiana, in the Atchafalaya Basin, when I found myself hauling it up a shallow stream: Rex was in the bow, all 300 pounds of him, making the stern go up in the air. It was an inefficient way to get things done, especially when we hit a log and I threw my back into it, pulling the canoe over it. The fiberglass hull cracked in three spots and the thwarts snapped in at least two. It's amazing we didn't sink to the bottom on the way back.

The second time was on the Chariton River in Missouri. Having been re-Bondoed and re-fiberglassed and re-patched for years, plus reinforced with 2 x 4s, that canoe now weighed as much as Rex. And due to the low water level, there were plenty of rocks and sandbars to cross. Again, I found myself dragging my canoe, crunching and cracking over debris, while Rex kicked back in the bow. By the time we made it to the pick-up spot, there was a foot of water in the Lümpenkraft.

Now, however, I had my father's aluminum canoe, so Rex and I headed out.

"We are gonna get that gar!" I told Rex, just like I told Robin the night before, and the night before that. "That gar is going down!"

"You might have to fish for ten years," Rex replied, "before you catch one like that again."

"So be it," I laughed. "There's nothing more important. The whole universe depends on it!"

Like usual, Rex was up front and I was in back, trying my damnedest to balance his girth. In addition to being a healthy hefty American, Rex was also six-foot-four. When he sat an inch to the right, I'd have to lean my mass to the left to counter balance. Sometimes I'd ask him to shift his position, but mostly I'd just try my best to deal with the imbalance.

Basically, Rex was highly unstable in a canoe—which I should've considered a bit more seriously, since he kept telling me he was jinxed. I wanted the company, though, and I was willing to put up with his ridiculous digging super-strokes. Rex paddled with great grunts and thrusts, as if battling the lake to show it who's boss. He also insisted on steering from the bow, when that's the work of the person in the stern. But I didn't argue or try to be a know-it-all by telling him what to do. I figured we'd get to where we were going, and then we'd get back.

But on the way back, after getting skunked for the fourth time trying to re-get that elusive gar, I decided we should check my limb-lines. So we made for the cypresses, where all my goldfish had been snatched by the stinking turtles.

That's when my poles starting brushing the branches. They were propped up behind me, sticking straight up. Then one got caught, so I reached up and grabbed them, to jerk them out of the way. Big Mistake! I suddenly had a treble hook lodged in my palm and Rex was spinning us in circles, trying to keep us away from the trees.

That sucker was sunk in there up past the barb, and I was so dang frazzled I couldn't think straight. While Rex paddled back, I wrassled my rods and got the offending one in front of me. It was my "special gar rod," an antique bamboo-looking job that I'd bought in a pawn shop up in Missouri. It had a World War II-era baitcasting reel, the pole was as thick around as my thumb, and I'd never caught a damn thing on it. It was probably meant for snagging paddlefish, but now it had snagged me.

When we got to the bank I got out my knife and cut the line. Rex pulled us up on the lawn and we went on into the house. Robin was watching reality TV, and since I didn't want to alarm her, I went straight to the sink to check the situation out. That bitch was in there and it wasn't coming out!

Last time I got stuck like this I was fourteen years old. After trying to reroute it with my father, then trying to push it up through my thumbnail, as well as back the way it came, we went to the doctor's office. I had to get three shots of Novocain so the doctor could wrench it out.

So that's what happened again. Robin took me to the emergency room, we waited around with all the drunk college kids sobering up from whatever antics that led to one of their friends getting his wrist slapped in a cast, and then the doctor called me in and asked me the exact same question the admitting nurse did:

"Well, did you catch anything?"

A week later I was ready to try again. That damn gar wasn't gonna get the best of me! Its ass was grass! It was time for me to teach it a lesson! In fact, on the example of my friend Catfish, I was even fixing on changing my name to Garfish. Because garfish were my totem fish! And I was gonna get that gar and claim my rightful state record!

The heat lightning was miles away when Rex and I got out to Gold Lake. When it flashed, we couldn't even hear the thunder. And since I often fish at night and see distant storms that never come near, I figured this one was at least a hundred miles away.

We dropped a couple of jug lines in. Each one had a concrete weight on one end, a plastic laundry detergent jug on the other, and fifteen or twenty feet of line. Between the weights and the jugs, each line had five to ten hooks, each rigged with a trotline minnow.

We also had our poles out. Rex had one up front and I had two in back. I had a plastic bottle full of gin and tonic, and he was drinking water. The sun was going down, some minnows were flipping on the surface, but nothing larger than sunfish were jumping.

Earlier that day, the temperature had been 105, and the heat index had been 113. It was in the upper eighties now, and all my flesh was sweltering. Plus, the mosquitoes were giving us hell—so we broke out the bug spray to ward them off. But since there was no wind at all, we kept sweating off the Off, and the mosquitoes kept dive-bombing us.

"Come on you state record gar!" I called out to the lake. "I know you're down there! I know you're hungry!"

"I thought you said it might be dead," Rex reminded me.

"He's gotta be out there," I shot back. "Or else I'm a fool, chasing nothing."

Rex laughed, and challenged me again:

"How do you know it's a he?"

"You're right," I replied. "It's probably a she, since the big ones are always female."

Then, as soon as the sun went down, the wind came up. Man, it came blowing in out of nowhere, straight up from Little Rock—a direction it never comes. Suddenly there were whitecaps all around us and the anchor was dragging behind the canoe.

"Screw the jugs," I told Rex, hauling up the bricks, "let's get the heck outta here!"

Instantly, it was like somebody turned out the lights. Everything went pitch black. Still, we could see the waves breaking around us, foaming and frothing two feet tall, lifting us up and slapping us down.

"Put your headlamp on!" I called to Rex, turning on my own.

We needed to see the stumps. We couldn't see the stumps. The wind was howling all around us, blowing in at 40 mph. There'd been no warning whatsoever. It was upon us.

"YEEEE-HAWWW!" I yowled, waves breaking over the bow. I was trying to make things seem less urgent as we paddled like lunatics, making for the shore.

Then we had to make a turn, and in doing so, we had to let the waves broadside us for a few minutes—which was okay, because they'd just lift us up and then we'd roll down the other side. Sometimes, though, they'd splash over the side. Big deal, we could take some water on.

Until, that is, we got T-boned by a freak three-footer, which bore us straight into a stump. I didn't even see it until we were on it. I figured we'd just roll with it.

But as the canoe listed to the left, Rex leapt to the right. I saw his mammoth silhouette rise, trying to compensate. All my instincts shrieked HUNKER DOWN! as the boat swung back to the right, Rex lurched the other way, and I couldn't believe it! In thirty-something years of canoeing, I have never capsized once, but now the canoe was rolling over and gallons of water were pouring in. Rex flopped into the drink, I followed, the boat turtled, and everything turned to Pure Chaos.

We were hanging on to the overturned canoe, thrashing in the water snakes, the alligator snapping turtles, the legion leeches, and all the lancelike logs sticking up around us. I managed to turn the boat over, though, and most of our gear was in it. Still, it was swamped.

"Let's swim!" Rex howled, his headlight bobbing up and down. "Forget this stuff!"

"No way!" I cried. "Let's make for those trees."

There was a stand of three or four cypresses twenty or thirty feet away. We started kicking, pushing the canoe. The waves were with us. We made it.

My most pressing concern was getting my tackle into a tree. I also wanted to tie up the canoe, so it wouldn't get away. The lake, however, was beating the crap out of me. It was slamming me into the canoe, and slamming the canoe into me, and getting rougher and rougher. I grabbed the tackle box, and then it opened. Tackle was spilling everywhere, but I got it shut and up on a limb, then pulled my way over to Rex.

He was having no luck lashing the bow-line to the trees and was hanging on while the waves kept bitchslapping him. In the meantime, the canoe had become a deadly weapon. With all that water in it, it was like a half-ton bucking bronco, leaping and lurching all over the place. Rex was struggling to hold it in place, and it kept jumping up and smashing down on us.

I got a hold of the rope, though, and managed to gather enough of it to haul around a tree. This took about five minutes, because the waves kept knocking me out of the lower branches, which I had to climb a bit to tie onto.

Eventually, I whooped up a knot and made my way down the canoe.

The lifejackets were floating away. I saw a paddle in the distance.

"Come on," Rex said, as a giant eely bottom feeder suddenly surfaced, surging over his arm, "let's get out of here!"

He was probably right, but I felt a sense of security in the trees.

"Just a second!" I yelled, then grabbed a paddle and put it in the limbs. I had to check on the rods, but there was a rope tangled around my foot. I couldn't tell if it was from my canoe or just some rope, but I managed to free myself. I also felt a trotline or two, abandoned by fishermen years ago. If either of us got caught in one of those, we could flounder and drown. But I didn't, and he didn't, and I saw that the rods were tangled in the net and that the net was tangled in a rope—so they'd probably stay there.

"Okay," I said, "let's stick together."

We struck out, my T-shirt and sneakers weighing me down. Rex had already shed his shoes. He was starting to pull ahead of me. I was exhausted, he wasn't. While I'd been swimming around and tying things up, he'd been conserving his strength by letting the canoe smack him upside the head.

I changed my course, making for another stand of cypresses. Rex called to me, but I couldn't answer. I couldn't waste my breath. Had to make it to those trees. Swallowing water, hitting logs—

I'd always been an excellent swimmer, but I'd never swam for my life. I'd also never had so much time to consider if this was finally it. For me, such thoughts usually occur in traffic, when accidents happen in a flash—which is comforting, almost, to never have time for terror to set in. But now it was definitely setting in.

I was wondering if I'd go down in my own lake, just a few blocks from home. Or if some vicious wave would hurl me into a log for the knockout. Or if I'd pass out, get sucked under, or end up as turtle food. Or would I have a heart attack? A stroke? Trying to survive—

Anyway, I made it to two trees forming a V and reached up and grabbed a limb. The waves were tossing me around like styrofoam, but I held on and saw Rex's light bobbing toward shore. It looked like half a mile, but I knew it couldn't be that far. He was gonna make it.

Wedging myself between the trees, I breathed hard, getting the air back into my lungs, trying to slow my heart rate down. The storm was still roaring in at a brutal speed, but I was safe in the cypresses, and no rain or lightning was coming down. It was all wind.

Then I saw Rex's light on the shore.

"Stay There!" he yelled. "I'm Going For Help!"

Still trying to recover, I didn't answer. I was trying to regain my wits. Besides, if I tried to answer, I'd be screaming into the tempest and I doubted my voice could even reach him.

So I clung, envisioning Rex bursting through the door sopping wet, telling Robin I'm clinging to a tree. Then I saw Robin in my mind, bolting up from the couch, not knowing what to do. Feeling helpless, feeling confused—almost as confused as me.

Because every minute I clung there gasping was a minute she'd be rushing around in turmoil, calling the cops, rousting the neighbors. Or maybe she'd try to launch the Lümpenkraft—which was beached on the lawn with giant cracks, completely unseaworthy and full of furious biting ants.

It would be totally stupid to swim for it, though, when I could just hold to that tree all night long. And as I clung and clung to that tree, trying to decide whether to go for it or hold out till the storm was over, I started to consider the most important existential stuff. Like whether I should change my ways in certain areas, which hardly matter now that I'm not clinging that tree. But at the time, I was thinking this could very well be it. Because basically, I was looking Death straight in the face, practically begging for a second chance.

Until I saw a ridiculous image: our cats, just sitting there. Yep, our tubby needy tuxedo cat Flossy with her patchy allergic fur, and our good golden tabby Gordon, the hardboiled hunter of mice and rabbits and lizards and things. They were just looking at me with their heads cocked, so I laughed.

I laughed because I wasn't seeing Robin, or my mother, or my father, or any human. I was only seeing two silly pets looking at me with funny expressions. So I figured this meant that maybe the situation wasn't as deadly as I was making it out to be—because if I really believed I was in danger, I wouldn't be seeing two goofy cats.

By now I'd been clinging for about ten minutes, and the storm wasn't getting any tamer. And since my breathing had evened out, and since it was obvious that I was gonna go for it, I took off a shoe. There was a knot in my other one, though, and I couldn't get it untied. Fuck that! With a surge of superhuman strength, I ripped that lace right out of it, then put my sneakers up in the tree.

All those swimming lessons as a kid, all those decades of swimming in lakes and rivers and pools—I'd been trained for this, I could do it. I'd swam this distance many times before.

But never in a maelstrom of limbs and logs and violent spray. But what else was I gonna do? Wait for the Sheriff to come out and get me? Boats, copters, EMTs? They'd probably gather a posse, then just wait for the storm to abate and come on out in a flat-bottomed boat. Then I'd be on the cover of the morning paper. The headline would read "Gar-Nut Rescued from Shallow Lake Less Than A Hundred Yards From Shore!" Or "Alcohol Involved in Foolish Boating Accident Raises Concerns About Local Professor!" Or "Some Scaredy Guy Whose Name Is Only Two Letters Away From Olympic World Champ Swimmer Too Afraid to Swim Like Rex Did!"

To hell with that! I was rested enough to take off my shirt and shoot out into the black. A log jammed me in the gut, but I kept on stroking blindly through the roiling night, waves smacking me in the face. I swam until I started hacking, then flipped onto my back.

The waves were body-checking me, body-slamming me, giving me the atomic drop. There were rusty hooks all around me, fishing lines, shrapnel, traps. At any time I could be thrown into some twisted tangle of chicken wire and bicycle spokes and barbecue grills with a thousand tentacles of tetanus reaching for my flesh. Not only that, but according to my exterminator, there were alligators in these waters over by Shit Creek.

"Ha," I actually laughed, "Shit Creek!"

Then suddenly there were stars above and I was swimming with the gars. Until, that is, I felt muck beneath my feet.

Standing up, I could see the shore only thirty feet away. I waded there, got up on the bank, made my way into the neighbor's field. My feet were bare and I was stepping on thistles—

Fuck It! More thistles, more sharp grasses. It was like stumbling on broken glass, coughing and wheezing as I went. Then I made it to the mounds. There were ant hills all around! Biting ants! Biting the crap out of me! But I kept on going and going and going—toward the street light beaconing my house.

Where a car was pulling out. It was Rex's Volvo station wagon. He was driving down the gravel road. Probably off to get a firetruck full of cops who'd be all pissed at me when they returned to find me on the couch tweezering thorns out of the bottom of my feet. So I blinked my headlamp at him, tried to signal him. But Rex couldn't see me in the field.

There was a wall of brambles in front of me. Blackberries, nettles, hornet nests. I could try to find a trail around it, or I could burst right through it. I don't know if I even stopped to think. The next thing I knew, I was a quarterback leaping a tide of linebackers, leading with his back.

I landed on the road, rolling in front of Rex's headlights. He stopped and stuck his head out the window.

"Hey," he asked, "want a ride back?"

We were forty feet from my front door.

"No," I said, trying to catch my breath, "I'll walk."

"Robin's at the neighbors," he said.

Woozy and fighting to stay upright, I couldn't see myself chasing after her, trying to find the exact neighbors she was collecting to rescue me.

"Honk three times," I told Rex. He did, and I heard Robin calling back.

But I didn't wait around. I thought I might collapse. Lungs heaving, heart hammering, I made for the door.

When I opened it up, the cats were there. Flossy was just looking at me with an oblivious expression, but Gordon knew something was up. He started meowing, and he kept on meowing as I went up the stairs, shedding soggy layers as I went.

I ended up in the shower, turning on the cold water. I didn't even touch the handle for the warm. I just sat down in the tub and let it rain down on all the lake crud and ant bites burning on me, while Gordon rushed back and forth, still crying in feline empathy.

I looked at my feet. They were scratched all to hell and starting to swell, but my pounding heart was settling down. It was like one of those times when you wonder if you should really be alive, because it could've gone the other way just as easily.

Last time I felt this way was in the middle of a Wyoming blizzard. I had crawled out of a wicked interstate wreck, concussions pounding all over my head, and for the next few days I couldn't help marveling at how lucky I was not to be dead meat. During that time, I never took one breath for granted.

Then I heard footsteps marching up the stairs.

"You're Never Going Fishing With Rex Again!" Robin yelled in a voice like I'm gonna get it. "I Forbid It!"

My mind, however, was on my state record gar—which I suddenly realized I didn't have to catch, not if trying like this can land me in situations like this. Because I don't have to prove anything to anyone! I had caught it, I had met it, and I knew this, and Robin knew this, and so does the fish—who I won't try to romanticize as being just as alive as me, just trashed and beat and trying to pull itself together. Nope, nobody knows what happened to that gar, and nobody will ever know.

Gordon, meanwhile, was stretched out on the linoleum—no longer wailing, no longer pacing, a strangely content look on his orange and white stripy face.

Photo of Mark Spitzer with his 106 lb., six-foot-five, alligator gar (© Eric Tumminia).

Contributors

Alison Baker is the author of two short story collections, *Loving Wanda Beaver* and *How I Came West, and Why I Stayed;* each was a *New York Times* Notable Book of the Year. Her fiction has received several O. Henry Awards. She was named 2001 Oregon Library Supporter of the Year by the Oregon Library Association, and has recently enjoyed residencies at both Ragdale and the Virginia Center for the Creative Arts. She and her husband, Hans Rilling, live in Rockbridge County, Virginia.

B.J. Best holds an MFA from Washington University in St. Louis. His first book, *Birds of Wisconsin,* is forthcoming from New Rivers Press in the fall of 2010. His recent chapbooks are *Drag: Twenty Short Poems about Smoking* (Centennial Press) and *State Sonnets* (sunnyoutside).

Randall Brown teaches at Saint Joseph's University & Rosemont College and holds an MFA from Vermont College. Recent work has appeared or is forthcoming in *Cream City Review, Quick Fiction, Connecticut Review, Saint Ann's Review, Evansville Review, Laurel Review, Dalhousie Review, upstreet, Gargoyle,* and others. He is the lead editor of *SmokeLong Quarterly* and the author of the award-winning collection *Mad to Live* (Flume Press, 2008).

Jerah Chadwick spent the last 26 years on the Aleutian island of Unalaska and has recently moved to Duluth, Minnesota. His latest book is *Story Hunger* (Salmon Publishing, Ireland) and he's recently had poems appear in *Alaska Quarterly Review*, *Alaska Reader* (Fulcrum), and *Crosscurrents North* (U of Alaska Press).

Ed Fischer, a research psychologist, is a native of Danbury, Connecticut. For the past 41 years he's lived in Glastonbury, near the state's best rock climbing sites. Two of his other articles about mountaineering and rock climbing were published in *Desert Exposure* and the *Manchester Journal Inquirer*.

Brent Fisk is a writer from Bowling Green, Kentucky. His work can be found in recent issues of *Boxcar Poetry Review*, *Greensboro Review*, and *Innisfree Journal*.

CB Follett is author of 6 books of poems, the most recent, *And Freddie is My Darling* (2009). *At the Turning of the Light* won the 2001 National Poetry Book Award; Editor/publisher of *Grrrrr, A Collection of Poems about Bears*, publisher and co-editor of *Runes*, a Review of Poetry (2001-2008), and general dogsbody of Arctos Press. She has several nominations for Pushcart Prizes, a Marin Arts Council Grant for Poetry, awards and honors and has been widely published.

Bart Galle is a medical educator and visual artist living in St. Paul, Minnesota. He is a 2008-2009 Loft Mentor Series Winner in Poetry and the winner of the 2008 *Passager* Poetry Contest for writers over 50. His poems have been nominated for a Pushcart Prize and *Best New Poets* 2009. They have appeared previously in *Minnetonka Review* and in *Water-Stone Review*, *The Comstock Review*, *White Pelican Review*, *Main Channel Voices*, *Coe Review*, *Eclipse*, and elsewhere.

Contributors

Stephen Graf lived in Madrid, where he worked for the public relations firm SEIS. He holds a Ph.D. in British Literature from University of Newcastle upon Tyne in England. He has been published in, among others: *Cicada, AIM Magazine, The Mountain Laurel, the Dana Literary Society Online Journal, The Southern Review, Mobius, The Chrysalis Reader, Fiction, New Works Review,* and *The Black Mountain Review.* He currently resides in Pittsburgh, Pennsylvania where he teaches English at Robert Morris University.

Peter Harris teaches at Colby College in Maine. He's published a chapbook, *Blue Hallelujahs.* His poetry has appeared in many magazines including, *The Atlantic Monthly , Epoch, Prairie Schooner, Ploughshares, Seattle Review,* and *Sewanee Review.* A former Dibner Fellow, he has been awarded residencies at Macdowell, the Guthrie Center, Red Cinder House, and The Virginia Center for the Creative Arts.

Alamgir Hashmi has published eleven books of poetry and several volumes of literary criticism in the United States, Canada, England, Australia, India, Pakistan, etc. He has won a number of national and international awards and honors, and his work has been translated into several European and Asian languages. For over three decades he has taught in European, Asian, and U.S. universities, as Professor of English and Comparative Literature.

Brandon Krieg grew up in Portland, OR. He is currently an instructor at DePaul University and Truman College in Chicago.

Eli Langner is a poet living in Tucson, AZ. His work has been published or is forthcoming in: *Sanskrit, The North American Review, descant, Red Wheelbarrow Literary Magazine, Celebrations, The Angry Poet, Bryant Literary Review, California Quarterly, Concho River Review, Confluence, Crucible, The Distillery, Fulcrum, Meridian Anthology Of Contemporary Poetry, Mother Earth Journal, The Old Red Kimono, The Owen Wister Review, Performance Poets Association Literary Review, Poetry @ The River Annual Review, SLAB, Steam Ticket, Veil: Journal of Darker Musings, Wisconsin Review,* and *Creations Magazine.*

Naton Leslie is the author of a book of narrative nonfiction, *That Might Be Useful* (Lyon Press, 2005), six volumes of poetry: *Their Shadows Are Dark Daughters* (1998) *Moving to Find Work* (2000), *Salvaged Maxims* (2002) *Egress* (2004) and *The Last Best Motif* (2004), and *Emma Saves Her Life* (2007). A collection of his short fiction, *Marconi's Dream and Other Stories* (2003) won the George Garrett Fiction Prize, and he is the recipient of fellowships from the National Endowment for the Arts and the New York Foundation for the Arts. He teaches writing and literature at Siena College, in Loudonville, New York.

Susan Lilley lives and teaches in Florida. Her collection, *Night Windows,* is the 2006 co-winner of the Yellow Jacket Press Chapbook Contest. She is a recipient of a Florida Individual Artist Fellowship and the 2009 winner of the Rita Dove Poetry Award (Salem College International Literary Awards). Her work has appeared or is forthcoming in journals such as *The Apalachee Review, Poet Lore, New Madrid, CALYX, Passager,* and *The Southern Review.* Her MFA in Creative Writing is from Stonecoast at University of Southern Maine.

Contributors

George Looney's books include *The Precarious Rhetoric of Angels* (2005 White Pine Press Poetry Prize), *Attendant Ghosts* (Cleveland State University Press, 2000), *Animals Housed in the Pleasure of Flesh* (1995 Bluestem Award), and the novella *Hymn of Ash* (the 2007 Elixir Press Fiction Chapbook Award). In addition, *Open Between Us*, a new book of poetry, is due out from the Turning Point imprint of WordTech Communications early in 2010. He is chair of the BFA in Creative Writing Program at Penn State Erie, editor-in-chief of the international literary journal *Lake Effect*, translation editor of *Mid-American Review*, and co-director of the Chautauqua Writers' Festival.

Denton Loving lives on a farm near the historic Cumberland Gap, where Tennessee, Kentucky and Virginia come together. He co-directs the Mountain Heritage Literary Festival at Lincoln Memorial University. His story "Authentically Weathered Lumber" received the 2007 Gurney Norman Prize for Short Fiction through the journal *Kudzu*. Other work has appeared in *Birmingham Arts Journal*, *Appalachian Journal*, *Somnambulist Quarterly*, *Heartland Review* and in numerous anthologies including *We All Live Downstream: Writings about Mountaintop Removal*.

Alexandria Marzano-Lesnevich lives in Cambridge, Massachusetts. She is currently completing her MFA in Nonfiction Writing at Emerson College, where she is working on a memoir about the law. Her short-short fiction appears online at *Storyglossia*, *Pindeldyboz*, and *Monkeybicycle*. Her essay "In the Fade," adapted from her memoir-in-progress, won the 2009 *Bellingham Review*/Annie Dillard Prize in Creative Nonfiction and is forthcoming from that publication in Spring 2010. For more information and links to other work, visit: *www.alexandria-marzano-lesnevich.com*.

Caitlin Militello is a writer and freelance editor living in suburban Buffalo, New York. Much of her work has been inspired by the 11 months she spent living in Japan: her short fiction piece, "Coming of Age," which appeared in the May 2009 issue of *Cha: An Asian Literary Journal*, has been nominated for *Best of the Net 2009*, and "An Unexpected Stop at Tama-reien," a work of non-fiction, is forthcoming in the August issue of *Cha*. In addition to creative writing, she writes and edits for the blogzine she founded, *The Talking Twenties*, and has had editorials published in English and Japanese on the *TalkingScience* blogs. She is currently working on a novel.

Martina Nicholson is a practicing Ob-Gyn in Santa Cruz, Ca. She is married, and has two teenage sons. She is interested in the emotional interior-scapes in women, and in the mysteries of the body and health; and how we find meaning in our lives. She has published two books of poems, *My Throat is Full of Songbirds*, and *Walking on Stars and Water*.

David Oestreich works as a human resources professional in Ohio where he lives with his wife and three children. His work has previously appeared in *Dash*, *Eclectica*, *Red Wheelbarrow* and *Ruminate*.

Robert Parham's recent work has been published by *The Oxford American*, *South Carolina Review*, *Shenandoah*, *Prairie Schooner*, *English Journal*, *Cincinnati Review*, *Atlanta Review*, *Baltimore Review*, *5 A.M.*, *Southern Review*, *Cimarron Review*, *Folio*, *Southern Quarterly*, and many other journals. Earlier work appeared in *Georgia Review*, *Southern Humanities Review*, *California Quarterly*, *America*, *Rolling Stone*, and a wide variety of other magazines. His chapbook *What Part Motion Plays in the Equation of Love* won the Palanquin Competition. He has published two other chapbooks. A collection of his poetry was a finalist for the Richard Snyder, *Main Street Rag*, *Snake Nation Press*, and the Marianne Moore poetry competitions. He presently edits the *Southern Poetry Review* and serves as Dean of the Katherine Reese Pamplin College of Arts and Sciences at Augusta State University.

Contributors

Carlos Reyes is a noted poet and translator. His latest book of poetry is *At the Edge of the Western Wave* (2004). His *The Book of Shadows; New and Selected Poems* is due out next year from Lost Horse Press. *A Suitcase Full of Crows* (1995) was a winner of the Bluestem Prize. His most recent book of translations is Ignacio Ruiz Pérez's *La señal del cuervo / The Sign of the Crow*. Last year he was recipient of The Fortner Award from St Andrews College. He has been an Oregon Arts Commission Fellow, a Yaddo Fellow, a Fundación Valparaíso Fellow, (Spain), a Heinrich Boll Fellow (Ireland) and most recently was poet-in-resident at the Joshua Tree National Park.

Nick Ripatrazone's recent work has appeared or is forthcoming in *The Kenyon Review, The Saint Ann's Review, Sou'wester, The Los Angeles Review, Mudlark,* and *The New York Quarterly.* He lives with his wife in New Jersey and is pursuing an MFA from Rutgers University.

Brian Shawver is the author of two novels, *The Cuban Prospect* and *Aftermath.* He is an associate professor in the English Department at Missouri State University, and a graduate of the University of Kansas and the Iowa Writers Workshop. He lives in Missouri with his wife, Pam, and their baby son, Simon.

Mark Spitzer grew up fishing for one-eyed monsters in the Mississippi River, but then lit out for Colorado, France, Louisiana, and ultimately, Arkansas—where he is now a prof. of creative writing. He has nine books out, most of them revolving around some sort of fish theme. He was recently featured as an expert on gar in the Animal Planet series *River Monsters.* For more info, see *www.sptzr.net.*

Donna Trump's writing career began in mid-life when she attended her first writing class, "Writing for the Absolute Beginner", at The Loft Literary Center in Minneapolis. In the ensuing four years she has taken many other classes at The Loft, participated in The Loft's Mentor Series for Emerging Writers, published poems and stories in *Speakeasy, Fog City Review,* and now, *Minnetonka Review.* She lives in downtown Minneapolis with her remarkably supportive husband and the occasional company of her two grown children. Donna continues her relationship with colleagues at The Loft, teaching and being taught in the country's oldest, largest and most comprehensive literary arts center.

A.D. Winans is the author of more than 45 published works of poetry and prose, which have been translated into eight languages. His work has appeared in over one thousand literary journals and anthologies.

He was the editor and publisher of *Second Coming* for 17 years. The archives of this award winning magazine and press are housed at Brown University.

His book, *The Land Is Not My Land,* was awarded a PEN Josephine Miles Award for excellence in literature. In 2005 a song poem of his was performed at New York's Tully Hall. He has been awarded editing, publishing, and writing awards from the National Endowment For the Arts, The California Arts Council, PEN, and the Academy of American Poets. Further information can be found at *www.adwinans.mysite.com.*

Robert E. Wood teaches in the School of Literature, Communication, and Culture at Georgia Tech. His film studies include essays on Fosse, DePalma, and Verhoeven, as well as *The Rocky Horror Picture Show.* He is the author of *Some Necessary Questions of the Play,* a study of Hamlet. His poetry has appeared recently in *Quiddity, Quercus Review , Blue Fifth Review, Ouroboros* and *Umbrella,* and is to appear in *War, Literature, and the Arts, Jabberwock Review, Blue Unicorn* and *Prairie Schooner.* A chapbook, *Gorizia Notebook,* from Finishing Line Press includes the poems presented here.

Minnetonka Review is an independent journal published twice annually on Lake Minnetonka, one of the largest lakes in Minnesota. The lake was first discovered by two children paddling up Minnehaha Creek from Fort Snelling. In 1852, Minnesota's territorial governor, Alexander Ramsey, named the lake after hearing the native Dakota people refer to it as minn-ni-tanka, which means "Great Waters." Soon thereafter, the first hotel was built on its shores and in 1855, Henry Wadsworth Longfellow made the area famous with his epic poem, "The Song of Hiawatha." Minnehaha, the heroine of his poem, was named after the creek that flows from Lake Minnetonka to become a tributary of the Mississippi. Minnehaha is the word for waterfall, or "laughing waters."

Through the far-resounding forest,
Through the forest vast and vacant
Rang that cry of desolation,
But there came no other answer
Than the echo of his crying,
Than the echo of the woodlands,
"Minnehaha! Minnehaha!"
All day long roved Hiawatha
In that melancholy forest,
Through the shadow of whose thickets,
In the pleasant days of Summer,
Of that ne'er forgotten Summer,
He had brought his young wife homeward
From the land of the Dacotahs;
When the birds sang in the thickets,
And the streamlets laughed and glistened,
And the air was full of fragrance,
And the lovely Laughing Water
Said with voice that did not tremble,
"I will follow you, my husband!"
In the wigwam with Nokomis,
With those gloomy guests that watched her,
With the Famine and the Fever,
She was lying, the Beloved,
She, the dying Minnehaha.
"Hark!" she said; "I hear a rushing,
Hear a roaring and a rushing,
Hear the Falls of Minnehaha
Calling to me from a distance!"

-Henry Wadsworth Longfellow
an excerpt from
"The Song of Hiawatha"

Lake Minnetonka

Minnetonka Review

In only its third year of publication, *Minnetonka Review* has already earned a national reputation for publishing entertaining, high quality fiction, nonfiction, and poetry in a well-designed and artful journal. Regarding our first issue, *NewPages.com* wrote "The maiden voyage of *Minnetonka Review* is a ride you must catch." *Literary Magazine Review* wrote "*Minnetonka Review* already has all the features of a more established literary magazine." We've had works reprinted in *The Best Creative Nonfiction* and named as Notable by *Best American Essays*.

We hope you've enjoyed reading this, our fifth issue, and we hope that you would like to be a part of our success! Please subscribe online, or send in the form below with a check or money order.

◯ I'll enjoy a one-year, two-issue subscription for $17.00.
(That will save me 30% off the cover price)

◯ I'll enjoy a two-year, four-issue subscription for $32.00.
(That will save me 33% off the cover price)

Name _____

Address _____

_____

Mail with check to:
Minnetonka Review / P.O. Box 386 / Spring Park, MN 55384